CAME HERE FOR MONEY?"

Nick said. "If you do, you're crazier than I thought."

Ithena lowered the bag. His eyes locked with Carter's.

"Power? If you want power, you could be *bawana* here. Or in Angola. Or Mozambique. I have influence in those places—and in others."

The African leader took three steps forward, smiling the contented half-grin that madmen can manage in moments of terror. He made a motion as if to open the door, but whirled around suddenly instead, lunging at Carter with the walking stick which had been converted into a long, very sharp dagger. . . .

NICK CARTER IS IT!

FROM THE NICK CARTER
KILLMASTER SERIES

NICK CARTER

KILLMASTER

The Blue Ice Affair

€

CHARTER BOOKS, NEW YORK

THE BLUE ICE AFFAIR

A Charter Book/published by arrangement with
The Condé Nast Publications, Inc.

PRINTING HISTORY
Charter Original/February 1985

ISBN: 0-441-06861-8

Charter Books are published by The Berkley Publishing Group,
200 Madison Avenue, New York, New York 10016.
PRINTED IN THE UNITED STATES OF AMERICA

Dedicated to the men of the
Secret Services of the
United States of America

PROLOGUE

The gusting wind blew sand and bits of gravel up from the low bluff of gray rocks where bulldozers and mechanical scrapers labored. Above them the sand dunes were piled nearly fifty feet high like walls guarding the moonscape of ravines and gullies where fortune upon fortune of diamonds still lay buried. There was always a sense of excitement and sacrilege to the mining operation at Oranjemund, Namibia. Bordered by the Orange River, the land they excavated had been reclaimed from the sea. The silt and rock that they scraped had existed for more than two hundred million years, and the terraces of bedrock they exposed one after the other would reveal diamonds formed a billion years before that. The operation, therefore, carried with it a sense of timelessness, the very same quality that the stones themselves conveyed. It is said, after all, that diamonds are forever.

The siren screamed once into the bowels of the pit. The heavy equipment ground slowly to a halt. The crust of millennia had been peeled away. Beneath the rutted Caterpillar treads lay a flat, smooth terrace eroded by the sea before man existed. Now, gangs of Ovambo tribesmen known as bedrock cleaners trotted down from the dunes. Dressed in waterproof orange caps with earmuffs, the blacks combed the depths of the site. They ran giant vacuums over the sheets of

1

stone, sweeping and sifting for anything vaguely resembling the clear, icy appearance of a diamond.

From atop the bulldozers, heads turned to observe the tribesmen at work. The eyes of the tour boss, a white South African, darted from one man to the next. Though the large majority of stones were found via fluoroscope amid the tons of crushed rock piled and later processed, many were found atop the terrace itself. Rewards were given for such finds, but despite every imaginable precaution, attempted thefts were common. The tour boss reconnoitered his area of the huge pit. His vigil was interrupted by the shouts and commotion of a cluster of workers. He watched as the Ovambo headman ran toward them. A discussion ensued. The headman turned to him, beckoning.

The tour boss walked to the men with a brisk, military cadence.

"What is it?" he demanded.

"A diamond, boss. The kind you been lookin' for. Blue—blue and clear like you wanted."

The South African sank to one knee. He scrutinized the exposed crown of the stone, then stood.

"Chip it out," he ordered.

The headman drew a bent metal spike and hammer from his leather satchel. He lay flat on the ground, studying the position of the diamond, then placed the thin metal spike to one side of it. Slowly he tapped at the rock that encircled it. He blew the sandy gravel away, then began working on its other side. By now, perhaps, fifteen workers had gathered, awaiting the results of his efforts. He probed the two sides of the gem with the instrument. It loosened. Gently he pried it from the terrace bedrock. His eyes widened as he took the five-carat stone into his hand. He looked up to the tour boss. The South African's hand was already extended. The tour boss held the diamond up to the pale sunlight. Even unpolished and unbuffed, its bluish hue was discernible. He nodded with no small degree of satisfaction.

"Tell your man we will have the stone weighed, then we will pay him his reward."

"Yes, boss," the headman agreed, translating the message.

The worker smiled broadly.

The tour boss walked hurriedly toward a Land-Rover parked at the northernmost corner of the pit. What he held in his hand was a type 11B boron-coated diamond, a stone indicative of a reserve that could change the course of satellite warfare forever.

Neville Burdon was no fool. It was for this reason that he had been entrusted with carrying the recently unearthed diamond samples through customs at Keniatta Airport in Nairobi to the people most interested in them. That is, those most willing to pay his price. He stood in the customs line now, the stones wrapped in a prophylactic and hidden where even the most ardent agent could never hope to find them. This was only as a precaution; his contacts in the Kenyan government were to meet him there and see to it that no search would happen. But in the profession of smuggling, no amount of precaution was inordinate. His brown hair had been dyed black. He had even grown a mustache for the occasion. Just in case. The line moved forward. It consisted mostly of businessmen, some from Africa, some from Europe and America. For the time being, he was one of them. An exporter of sorts.

The Englishman lifted his bags. He moved them forward. No sooner had they touched the floor again than two Kenyan government officials, dressed in dark suits, walked to him.

"Mr. Burdon?" one of them inquired politely.

"Yes?"

"You will come with us, please."

The other, the larger of the two, took his bags. He was home free. His contacts had come through.

The three men walked through the modern airport. Constructed in 1976 by an Italian architectural firm at a cost of millions, the Kenyan government elected to default on payments several months after its completion. The architect was expelled from the country penniless. He committed suicide shortly thereafter, Burdon recalled. It was a story he remembered, for this was Africa, a continent where anything was possible, where even thieves and spies had to be constantly on guard. Once outside, the three climbed into a waiting limousine bound for the Nairobi Hilton. The black sedan wended its way from the major highway leading into the city to streets lined with modern office buildings that contrasted with the poverty-level housing and poorly dressed natives. The anomaly of Africa, Burdon mused. Before him, huge cranes stood at the bases of half-finished structures incomplete not for lack of money, but because the government could find so few workers skilled in the operation of heavy equipment. Here, the culture of magic and superstition existed side-by-side with the nuclear age.

A valet opened the back door to the limo when it came to a halt before the swank, American-owned Hilton hotel. Burdon and his two escorts exited. They entered the hotel, then took an elevator to the seventh floor. It was in Room 714 that his prospective buyers waited.

One of the Kenyans rapped on the door. It opened after a moment's hesitation. A thin, well-dressed man of Slavic descent appeared. He bobbed his head as if to confirm the details of some tacit prearrangement. With that, the two government officials walked off, leaving Burdon smiling with his hand extended.

"Neville Burdon. I believe you're expecting me."

The Russian accepted his handshake.

"Vladimir Andrei. Come in," he answered.

Burdon entered. Inside were two faces he immediately recognized: Boris Troyansky, a gemologist he had dealt with once before, and Colonel Theo Ithena, leader of the South-West African People's Organization, SWAPO. He had seen Ithena's photograph in the newspaper.

The social amenities were nonexistent.

"Well, then, shall we get down to business?" Burdon asked.

The gemologist rose.

4

"You have the diamonds?"

"Of course."

"May we see them, please?" he said, more a demand than a question.

Burdon reached into the back of his mouth. He clasped his thumb and forefinger around a section of bridgework, then clicked it loose. Slowly he drew on a thin plastic thread leading down his throat to his stomach.

"Your diamonds," he said, a note of triumph in his voice as he produced the parcel of tiny stones.

Troyansky put his hand forward. Burdon didn't move.

"First, my fee."

The gemologist looked to Andrei, who frowned.

"Here," Andrei snapped at last, handing him an envelope.

Burdon handed the parcel over. Even before he began counting the ten one-thousand-dollar bills the envelope contained, Troyansky was examining the gems through a 10X loupe at the far end of the room. Both Ithena and Andrei were huddled around him.

"Are they real?" Andrei asked impatiently.

The gemologist waved him off. He put the loupe down, then placed the largest of the diamonds in a crucible that was mounted above a lattice of transistors and electrical components. Troyansky donned a pair of smoke-gray glasses.

"You will look away now," he advised, about to submit the stone to an electrical conductivity test.

He flicked a switch to turn it operational. Within seconds, the blue stone appeared in the crucible as a silvery-white orb.

Troyansky studied a meter set to the side of the device as Ithena and Andrei looked on.

He flicked the switch to its "off" position.

"Yes? What is it?" Andrei asked urgently.

"They are real," he answered simply.

A feeling of gratification welled within all present in the room.

"Well, gentlemen, if you're satisfied, I shall be on my

way," Neville Burdon said.

Andrei looked at him with stony eyes.

"I think not, Mr. Burdon," he said, raising a silenced Walther P-38 from his belt. He fired the weapon twice. It struck his victim in his upper torso through the heart. Burdon dropped to the floor, dead in an instant.

The Russian replaced the gun in its holster, then turned with a smile.

"Colonel Ithena, I think it's time we talked business," he said to the SWAPO leader.

ONE

The telephone sounded three sharp rings jarring enough to wake Nick Carter from even this deepest of slumbers. A rest well deserved, considering the night before. He plucked the receiver from its cradle. It might have weighed fifty pounds.

"Yeah?"

The voice at the other end offered no respite, night before notwithstanding.

It was David Hawk, his gruff voice more demanding than any phone or morning alarm.

"I need to see you right away."

"Ah, it's always so nice to hear from you, sir." He cast a sidelong glance at the blonde who snuggled up to him from behind.

"Spare me the sarcasm. I know what time it is, but this can't wait. You've got a reservation on the ten o'clock flight from Kennedy to Dulles. Be on it. I'll be expecting you by noon."

Carter looked at the clock that sat on the hotel night table. It was exactly 6:01 A.M.

"Yes, sir," he muttered.

With those words and an abrupt click of the phone, a three-day whirlwind romance begun on Friday in Las Vegas ended in New York. It was a sad excuse for what was to have been a month-long vacation. The girl beside him sighed as if cognizant of his plight. Her soft hand stroked his bare chest as she slept. *The old man has some sense of timing*, Carter thought, torn between the bed's warmth and an overriding sense of duty. *Okay, okay, the vacation's over*, a voice inside him urged, the voice of his more professional instincts. He rose. It was these same instincts that told him something was up. Something big that Hawk felt he could not entrust to any but the most seasoned of AXE agents.

Carter walked to the bathroom and doused his face with cold water. His last mission had been in Libya, and it had been a bitch. Looking into the mirror before him, he hoped that what Hawk had in mind now was in a less volatile area of the globe. He began shaving, knowing that this was too much to ask. In his profession, there was no room for piece-of-cake assignments. He was paid and paid damned well to take on the tough ones. Still, North Africa was a long shot. Agents were rarely sent to the same region of the world back-to-back for fear of blowing their cover. Where would he be sent? The question had his juices flowing. He ran the razor across his face. There had been rumors circulating through the corridors of AXE headquarters for weeks regarding covert action in Poland, but it involved mostly propaganda to egg on the Solidarity movement. Stuff like that was usually handled by caseworkers for the CIA. He cleaned the razor under running water. No, this was something more. There was an urgency to David Hawk's voice that told him that something was breaking fast and not in the controlled fashion of events in Eastern Europe where both Soviet and Western agents had been in place for decades. Carter guessed he would have to wait. Some things never changed. Regardless of seniority, an agent never knew exactly where he was going until the last possible moment. He washed the remnants of shaving cream from his face, then buried his head in a towel.

Carter walked into the next room. He dressed, then packed the few personal articles he had brought with him to New York. He glanced into the mirror above the bureau. Already he was feeling better and eager to return to Washington. Behind him, his blond friend was still sleeping, a tanned thigh peeking from beneath the white bed sheets. There was no question the moment was ripe for a session of morning lovemaking. He sighed wistfully, then took a pen from his inside jacket pocket.

"Good-bye, angel," he scribbled on a piece of hotel stationery. "It's been great."

DuPont Circle in Washington was buzzing with the usual traffic and midmorning commotion as Nick Carter left his cab, then slipped the driver a five. He entered the Amalgamated Press and Wire Services Building more curious than ever to learn the reason for Hawk's early-morning wake-up call. He boarded the elevator and pushed the button for the floor where Hawk had his office. Unlike the CIA building in Langley, Virginia, he could not expect to encounter the assortment of old cronies and burnt-out agents who walked the corridors there, but rather a near deserted floor where security was so tight even he would be asked to register an AXE ID and serial number at the main clearance desk. The elevator came to a halt. The doors opened with a mechanical hum. He stepped out. It was Joe Larkin, one of AXE's newest recruits, a bright young man recently graduated from Georgetown Law School. He smiled from behind his desk.

"Didn't think you'd be back so soon, Nick," he said.

Carter handed him a card. Larkin ran it under the ultraviolet light. Its electromagnetic digits registered for clearance.

"I didn't think I'd be back so soon either."

Larkin gave him the go-ahead.

"He's expecting you."

Carter walked down the corridor to David Hawk's office, then tapped lightly on the door.

"Come in," Carter heard him mutter.

He opened the door. AXE's director looked as if he hadn't slept in two days. His desk was covered with cables and telegrams. He was poring over a series of maps as Carter entered.

"Close the door," Hawk said without looking up.

He did, approaching Hawk's large desk with the kind of reverence his boss inspired. In his sixties, short, squat, and tough as a bulldog, David Hawk was something of a legend among covert operatives. One of the founding fathers of AXE, he had masterminded some of America's most stunning undercover triumphs. The reality of the matter was this: when a situation was too hot for the CIA, it was left with AXE. No questions asked. No directives given. Just the verbal order, occasionally emanating from the President himself: "Handle it."

Carter took a seat before Hawk's desk. A cigar was lit and burning in his ashtray. From the mound of ashes, Carter was now positive his boss had been there all night. Finally, Hawk looked up.

"Sorry to call you in like this, Nick. I know what you went through on your last assignment, but this couldn't be helped."

"I understand, sir."

"You have disengaged yourself from any commitments, any individuals who might be expecting to see you over the next couple of months?"

"Yes, sir."

Hawk nodded.

"Good."

He took his cigar from the ashtray and looked at Carter, puffing as if assessing his top man's physical and mental condition. Hawk had once told Carter that ninety-five percent of other agencies' failed missions—which AXE eventually cleaned up—could be directly attributed to agent fatigue. He seemed pleased with what he saw.

"Nick, a rather messy situation is developing in Namibia that must be handled right away. Because of our delicate relationship with South Africa and the emerging black African nations, the CIA would prefer that it be taken care of by us."

"I understand."

Again Hawk nodded, puffing on his cigar.

"I knew you would," he said, then pushed forward a map.

"This is a map of the region. As you know, Namibia has been under the jurisdiction of South Africa since a League of Nations mandate in 1920. More recently, in 1973 to be exact, the United Nations Court of Justice overturned that mandate, ruling that the South African presence was illegal and demanding free elections for an independent nation of Namibia. That ruling has, of course, been roundly ignored."

"I'm aware of that. I'm also aware that SWAPO, the terrorist organization, has been fighting to liberate Namibia ever since."

"Right. And that brings us to the messy situation I mentioned earlier."

Hawk took a cable from his desk top.

"An urgent message was passed along to my office from a CIA caseworker in South-West Africa this Thursday. It was sent weeks ago, but now it's in our laps. It states that a major diamond reserve has been discovered in the Oranjemund province of Namibia by Consolidated Diamond Mines, a branch of De Beers."

Carter shrugged. "That's already one of the richest diamond-producing areas in the world. What's the catch?"

Hawk sighed wearily. He fell back in his chair as if the hours of sleeplessness had finally caught up with him.

"These are more than just diamonds, Nick. They're boron-coated blue diamonds. Type eleven-B, if you want the scientific jargon. High conductivity. High resistance. They're used in the making of laser beam weaponry."

"But South Africa is one of our staunchest allies. With Namibia still under their control, the U.S. is sure to be the beneficiary of a find like that."

Hawk snorted.

"Unfortunately, it's not that simple. I've been trying to piece together the shreds of intelligence we've managed to get our hands on, and it's shaping up like this: it's my opinion that the Soviets are making a move to gain control of those reserves."

11

"But how?"

"By staging a coup. By using SWAPO to spearhead the drive, the Russians are going to back an invasion of Namibia." He pointed to the westernmost region of the map. "Arms shipments have already been detected coming into Moçâmedes, a seaport in Angola. At the moment, there are between seven and ten thousand Cuban troops throughout the country. For all we know, they could be part of this too. One way or another, we need to know when this offensive is going to be launched and its intensity. More than that, we have got to prevent any shift in the current political balance from occurring."

Carter considered Hawk's words for a moment.

"If this invasion is going to happen, there must be Russian advisors coordinating it. It wouldn't be like the Soviets to go about this haphazardly."

"They haven't. Vladimir Andrei of the KGB is chief of the SWAPO task force. He and a Cuban named Carlos Ramirez are the brains behind the movement. Their logic is simple. If they can take over Namibia by force, a puppet will be installed. That would be SWAPO's leader, Colonel Theo Ithena. If they can't, they hope to disrupt productivity at the Oranjemund mine through guerrilla attacks, thus tying South Africa—and perhaps the United States—in a Vietnam-type conflict. No winners. Just a lot of bad international press for us and a halt to production of the gems. Either way, the U.S. is the loser."

Carter cast his boss a long stare. Something wasn't adding up, and before he left the States he needed to know the entire story with no details left out, no surprises he would have to live with later.

"Forgive me, but there's one thing I don't get."

"What's that?" Hawk rasped.

"The South African army is one of the best trained and equipped in the world. If they wanted to, they could rout both SWAPO and the Cubans simply by invading Angola before the Russians gained a foothold. You can't tell me that they don't have the same intelligence we do.''

Hawk tossed Carter a dossier. Stamped on it was the most secret of AXE codes.

Carter looked it over quickly. It contained sworn statements from the leaders of SWAPO and the Angolan government outlining atrocities committed by mercenary soldiers during a recent South African raid into Angola. They weren't very savory.

"Colonel Ithena will be presenting this to the U.N. Court of Justice next week," Hawk said. "Many of those victims were Angolan civilians. Ithena is going to ask for a total economic boycott on trade with South Africa because of it. Even an economy as strong as theirs couldn't hope to withstand sanctions like that. The South African government is walking on eggshells at the moment.''

Carter tossed the dossier back onto Hawk's desk. A look of disgust had crept across his features.

"And that's the regime we're supporting?''

Hawk rarely talked about two things. One of them was his personal life. The other was philosophy. Still, he was pensive now as he hesitated, then spoke at last in a soft voice.

"That isn't our concern. You've worked with mercenaries before. Some are adventurers in search of a buck, others psychotic killers who should be tried in court for what they are. Your mission here is to see that those diamonds don't fall into the hands of the Soviets. Nothing more, nothing less. I knew this assignment was going to be a little gray around the edges. That's why I insisted that you take it on. But as long as we're on the subject of atrocities, maybe you'll want to take a look at these.''

Hawk handed Carter a series of photographs dated over the past two months.

"The result of explosions from incendiary devices planted by SWAPO in schools, post offices, and government buildings throughout South Africa and Namibia. Thirty-eight in the last sixty days, Nick. At last count, seven deaths and twenty-three permanently injured. Africa is hot. Both sides

13

feel they're fighting for what's rightfully theirs. There are no good guys or bad. We know only that SWAPO is being supported by the Kremlin. If they win, we lose much more than we can afford to.''

"And these boron-coated diamonds. They're worth that much to the Russians?''

Hawk was never more serious.

"They could change the course of satellite warfare for decades to come, Nick. In fact, they'd probably risk war over them.''

Carter nodded, feeling the adrenaline stir inside him.

"You'll get your information, sir. What's more, if there's any way to do it, this coup will be thwarted before it ever begins.''

TWO

The flight from Washington to Johannesburg, South Africa, is approximately twenty-one hours plus a one-hour layover on the tiny Portuguese island of Isla de Sol for refueling, this due to a flight plan that must skirt every other African nation or risk having the plane shot from the air. To call the trip draining is an exercise in understatement. It was for this reason that Carter elected to check into his hotel almost upon landing at Jan Smuts Airport before making his way to Pretoria the next morning. His sleep was sound and dreamless. He rented a Mercedes in the hotel lobby, then took the two-hour drive to South Africa's capital feeling refreshed and even excited about meeting Major General Van der Grif.

In the early seventies, Carter had been active in the Congo, working with a team of South Africans and their protégés in stabilizing the existing regime against Simba rebels. The mission had been a success, and during that stint he'd come to respect the discipline and earnest professionalism of the Afrikaaner intelligence network. But events had altered the stability of their country now. With military campaigns being waged on the borders of Mozambique, Angola, and Botswana, South Africa was literally surrounded by Communist nations. Their only buffer, their line of reasoning went, was Namibia—a province they adamantly refused to relinquish.

Signs of the tension were everywhere. Even as he drove up the N1 highway, two-ton military trucks, jeeps, and artillery made their way toward the northern borders where sporadic fighting continued. From the N1, he took Route 9 leading into the city and away from the nearly one hundred miles of desolate plains that separated Johannesburg from Pretoria.

Once in the city, Carter took Hamilton Street straight to the Union Buildings complex, an awesome sight to anyone unfamiliar with its grandiose yet stolid architecture. Tier upon tier of lavish gardens and sweeping lawns lead up to the Union Buildings, South Africa's governmental offices, where a thirty-foot statue of Karl Krueger stands overlooking the entire city. The complex itself, done in a modified Greek Revival style, appeared to Carter like something out of Disneyland. It was totally in keeping with the vision Afrikaaners had of their society. Powerful. Impenetrable. But today, Carter thought as he approached the very symbol of their strength, the South African society seemed almost fragile.

He drove his Mercedes to the fourth and highest tier. Two military policemen greeted him. Once he'd explained himself, they took his car and allowed him to enter. He registered with security in the main lobby, then proceeded to Van der Grif's office on the second floor.

The Office of National Security was large and surprisingly quiet when he entered. A secretary took his name, then buzzed the major general on the intercom. Seconds later, the door swung open and there stood Karl Van der Grif, head of South African national security, arms spread enthusiastically.

"Mr. Carter! How good to see you! And how opportune. We were only this morning talking about our friend from the United States."

He offered his hand, smiling as if they'd known one another for years. Carter accepted, of course, but his smile was only polite.

"I decided to stay overnight in Joburg. The flight here was a long one."

"Of course, of course," Van der Grif agreed, his eyes twinkling behind a pair of gold-rimmed glasses.

A large, strapping man in his late forties, Van der Grif appeared friendly, almost jovial. His precisely groomed hair and impeccable dress seemed somehow pretentious, as if the camouflage khakis he had no doubt worn years before were better suited to his looks.

Carter followed him into his office. They sat. Van der Grif opened a wooden box containing cigarettes, which Carter declined.

"A cigar, perhaps?" he asked, waving toward a humidor to the side of his desk.

Carter smiled wryly.

"Major Van der Grif, I appreciate your hospitality, but I'm not here to pay a social call, nor am I a politician who will go back to the States praising or condemning your country. I'm here acting on behalf of the United States on a matter we consider critical: the Oranjemund diamond mine."

The South African's smile faded slowly. It was replaced by a colder, sterner expression. His eyes lost their twinkle. They now appeared deadly serious.

"Very well, Mr. Carter. Shall we begin at the beginning? There's a closed security council meeting in progress now. If it suits your schedule, I'd like you to sit in on it for a while."

"That would be fine, Major. Time is at a premium."

Van der Grif flicked on his intercom.

"Miss Brand, please inform security that Mr. Carter and I will be arriving at the council meeting momentarily." He looked at his visitor squarely. "Shall we?"

Carter rose, and they both left the office for the high-ceilinged corridors of the second floor. Van der Grif gave a nod to the military police who stood outside the chamber doors. One of the soldiers swung the door open. They entered.

Inside was a large oblong table complete with headphones and simultaneous translating equipment; none of it was in use today, however, since those in attendance were exclusively

South African. Before the group, a young woman was explaining a series of charts documenting the Oranjemund excavation. She threw Carter a glance from the podium. A rumble of speculative whispers followed from among the group, then ceased after Carter and the major sat down. Still, that glance—so brief but so intense—stayed with him. Even from a distance, Carter could see that her blue eyes were dazzling, her features chiseled and refined. A more beautiful geologist he could not have hoped for.

"The type eleven-B boron-coated diamond is in many ways a freak of nature," she said, beginning again. "Its scarcity can be illustrated when one considers that in existing diamond mines two hundred and fifty tons of kimberlite rock yield just half a carat of polished diamond. Gems of the boron-coated variety are far less prevalent. In fact, since the element boron is found only in combination with other elements, it is among the rarest found in nature."

Carter turned to Van der Grif as their lecturer continued.

"Who is she?" he whispered.

"Aubrey Erhardt. She's a geologist. Our government has commissioned her and a team of others to document the find and estimate its magnitude."

"She's beautiful."

Van der Grif studied him, then shook his head.

"Americans," he muttered.

Carter watched as Aubrey Erhardt explained the origins of the Oranjemund find.

"The boron-coated diamond is formed in much the same way as a normal diamond. Within the earth's crust there is a gradual increase in temperature as the depth increases, so that when sufficient depth is reached, the temperature is high enough to cause the melting of the rock itself. In the case of diamonds, this molten rock occurs at even greater depths and in combination with extraordinary pressure. During the earth's formation a rock known as kimberlite was created, and within the kimberlite, combinations of elements gathered in tiny pockets. It was out of this compounding of chance elements that diamonds were formed. In the case of the type eleven-B stone, not only did this series of events take place, but another rare element was present at exactly the right temperature and at exactly the right moment: the trivalent metaloid called boron.''

"All very interesting, Miss Erhardt,'' one of the men interrupted, "but perhaps you can tell us the significance of these stones. Surely there's more to these diamonds than jewelry!''

The remark brought a chuckle from those at the table, but the young geologist was not amused.

"No, these are not for jewelry. The unique characteristics of the blue type eleven-B diamond were only discovered in the late 1950s by a group of German scientists working under the late Wernher von Braun. At that time, it was theorized that laser beams could be used as weapons. Their intense heat could not only destroy matter, but when magnified to their purest form, they could disintegrate it at the speed of light and at distances of thousands upon thousands of miles—even light years. The reason I use the word theorize is because the only resistors capable of carrying energy in that ultraconcentrated form were boron-coated. Since there was no supply in existence at that time, the project was abandoned. Until now.''

Another man, this one in uniform, raised his hand.

"Are you saying that in all the world, there is no other source for these diamonds outside of Oranjemund?''

The young woman's blue eyes fixed upon him.

"Just one—in the Siberian province of Yakutia, between the Lena River and the Arctic Circle. Unfortunately for the Russians, the average winter temperature there is minus fifty degrees Fahrenheit. Not only are the rivers frozen, but steel becomes brittle, brake fluid freezes, and rubber crisps like potato chips in that climate. The prospects of mining are almost nil.'' She cast him a quick, significant smile. "Outside of that, gentlemen, Namibia represents the only source in the world for these stones.''

A heavy silence followed her remarks. Her presentation had come to an end on a note of drama that seemed impossible to escape. The future of the free world could well depend upon who maintained access to the rarest of rare stones.

"Thank you for your time, Miss Erhardt," Van der Grif said. "You will excuse us for the time being?"

"Of course," she answered, gathering her charts and notes as Carter's eyes stayed on her. She noticed his stare. If he were not mistaken, it was something close to a smile that she offered as their eyes met. She left the room in silence, and Major General Van der Grif assumed her position at the podium.

"Gentlemen, before we continue with this meeting, I would like to introduce to you an advisor sent to us from the United States. His name is Nick Carter."

The seven men at the table turned to him. Some seemed skeptical, others visibly relieved to see a show of U.S. interest.

Carter rose halfway. "Thank you. It's good to be here." He glanced around him. Before each man was a nameplate and title. They ranged from diplomats to military officers. There could be no doubt that these were the most trusted and powerful men in the South African government.

"I think it's important that Mr. Carter be briefed on every facet of the Oranjemund situation," Van der Grif said, then turned to Carter. "You know about our recent problems in Namibia?"

"Yes."

"And SWAPO?"

"I know who they are and why they want independence. I also know that with this recent find, the stakes have gone up considerably. Our best information has the Soviets backing SWAPO, with guerrilla raids into Namibia likely."

"Your information is correct. And now that the significance of the diamonds has been explained, I trust you see the urgency of this matter."

"I do," Carter retorted, "and my government is committed to doing everything possible, short of military intervention, to prevent them from falling into the hands of the Russians.''

Carter reached to the side of his chair and produced a file from his attaché case. In it were photographs of four men. One of them was very dead. He passed copies around the table.

''The picture marked number one is of Neville Burdon, an international smuggler. As you can see, Mr. Burdon met with an untimely end. His mutilated body was found in a ditch just outside of Nairobi. Though it was made to appear he'd been robbed by a band of natives, a close examination of the morgue photo reveals two bullet wounds above the heart. Our people have reason to believe it was Burdon who smuggled samples of the stones found in Oranjemund to Soviet agents. He was killed to maintain secrecy.''

Each of the officials scrutinized the dead man's photo. Confident that no one took exception to his conclusions, Carter continued.

''The three additional photographs are of the men we believe are behind the SWAPO task force: Vladimir Andrei of the KGB, Carlos Ramirez, a Cuban military advisor, and your own Colonel Theo Ithena of the South-West African People's Organization. If the Russians have their way, Namibia will be 'liberated' with Colonel Ithena as its president.''

Seymour Jenkins, who headed South Africa's diplomatic corps, could not contain himself.

''Mr. Carter, I would like to take exception to the word liberate. Namibia has been under the jurisdiction of our country since 1884. That occupation was validated in 1915 and again in 1920 by the League of Nations. It has remained in effect ever since.'' He turned to the others for support. ''I should think the word 'invade' is more justified in this situation than 'liberate.'''

Carter tried his best to be diplomatic in answering. Yet in the back of his mind he could not help but remember the epithet used by blacks to describe these people: "rocks." They were stubborn, and on the subject of Namibia it had reached the state of a national neurosis.

"I'm not here to discuss politics, Mr. Jenkins. As far as I'm concerned, this is your country. Run it as you like. What I am here to do is to prevent a Soviet invasion from happening."

"Yes," Van der Grif agreed, "and we're all anxious to hear how you intend to do it."

The tone of his voice was harsh and authoritarian. Carter didn't like it.

"Apparently not with a great deal of your help," he snapped back. "As I understand it, this situation has gotten rather international, hasn't it, Major?"

The men at the table seemed to bristle at his response. Carter had learned early that the Afrikaaners' first strategy in dealing with foreigners was that of intimidation. But once they saw that someone wasn't about to submit to it, their tune changed.

As Carter suspected, Van der Grif's countenance softened a shade. He took a newspaper from the table and held the headline up for all to see. It read "U.N. to Meet on Worldwide Economic Boycott of South Africa."

"Mr. Carter is obviously referring to SWAPO's report on mercenaries in Angola," Van der Grif said in a quiet voice. "To answer your question, yes. This affair has gotten very international. To be frank, our hands are tied. If we are to survive this U.N. vote and rally at least some support, there can be no further violations of the territorial borders of our neighbors. To do otherwise would be tantamount to suicide."

"Are the charges true?"

The major general squirmed. He shot swift glances to the seven others gathered around him.

"Yes," he finally answered. "The men we recruited to fight in Angola were apparently overzealous. The atrocities were committed, but without our sanction. None of us here deny responsibility."

Carter nodded.

"Then let's get to the task at hand. With a counterattack into Angola ruled out, we are forced to deal with only the major players: Andrei, Ramirez, and Ithena. If we can neutralize those men, no invasion will be possible."

The man in uniform, Colonel Coetzee, looked up glumly from the tabletop.

"That is easier said than done. I'm afraid our contacts inside Angola have been deteriorating steadily since the late seventies. A team of our best men was sent in on a reconnaissance mission one week ago. Their orders were to keep in UHF contact daily. We haven't heard from them in two days."

"Dead?"

"We have no way of knowing. Scattered. In hiding, perhaps. In either case, we can only assume the mission has failed. With the degree of technology available to the Angolan military—and with Russian advisors there to show them how to use it—even high-altitude reconnaissance is impossible. Two of our planes have been shot down in the past month."

"I see."

"Colonel Coetzee raises an interesting subject," Jenkins intoned. "We were hoping your country's satellite photographs of Angola might be made available to us."

Carter considered his proposal. It seemed reasonable.

"I will cable my people regarding your request. Unofficially, I see no reason why they'd be denied us. We're going to need all the information we can get."

"Bravo, Mr. Carter! Bravo!" the South African cheered.

The others at the table were sullen at Jenkins's display of his English heritage. Though people of English descent accounted for better than one third of the white population, the Afrikaaners considered even them outsiders.

Carter smiled inwardly.

"There is something else," he said by way of conclusion. "Since we agree that members of your military cannot be used in any operation inside Angola, I will be totally in

23

charge of this undertaking.''

Carter's eyes darted to Van der Grif, then to each of the men around him.

"Agreed," the major general replied.

"I will need access to weapons. That includes handguns, mortars, machine guns, and explosives."

Again he paused.

"Agreed."

"The personnel used in any raid that might be undertaken will be selected by me and will answer directly to me. There will be an unlimited budget for salaries, blandishments, or whatever else I deem necessary in completing this mission successfully."

"We agree to all of that," Jenkins's voice rang out. "But exactly what is it you plan?"

"That will depend on what we're up against, Mr. Jenkins. As I see it, there are only two possibilities aside from all-out war. One is a tactical raid whereby the principal figures backing the movement are kidnapped or in some other way neutralized. The other is a diplomatic course of action. That would involve giving SWAPO a voice in the government of Namibia but retaining South Africa's right to the Oranjemund mine."

Colonel Coetzee guffawed.

"Mr. Carter, SWAPO is backed entirely by the Soviets. They supply them with weapons, complex military technology, even Cuban troops! To give them a voice would be to turn the government over to them. The Oranjemund mine would be in the hands of the Russians within months. Please remember that the support we can expect from the U.S. is understandably shallow due to our policy of apartheid. The Soviets are not so concerned with this. They will take over the province given the slightest opportunity."

Carter rubbed a hand along his rugged jaw.

"Then that leaves us with just one possibility, doesn't it, gentlemen?"

He rose.

"Major Van der Grif, I will send that cable now if you don't mind."

He left as the conference room erupted in debate. Most had heard what they wanted to hear. The United States had stood by, ineffectively shadow boxing the Russian bear, while Angola and Mozambique had turned Communist. Here, the line would be drawn. Though the U.S. was unwilling to commit troops, Carter had carte blanche to do what was necessary.

Carter waited in the corridor for a few idle moments, wondering whether Hawk could indeed come up with the satellite photos that seemed so necessary. Inside, he could hear Jenkins's nasal whine over the garble of voices as the seven men engaged one another. In the end, he knew they would have no alternative but to give him what he wanted.

He strolled down the corridor to Van der Grif's office feeling suddenly stale. It wasn't the remnants of yesterday's jet lag; it was more like the ennui that comes during the opening phases of planning a major mission. He wanted to square the details as soon as possible, then get on with it. Leave politics to the politicians. Give him the men, the weapons, and the problem. Strategy and execution of the plan, that was his cup of tea.

The door to Van der Grif's office was open. Inside, Aubrey Erhardt was going over the notes of her lecture with a secretary. Each of the men present would receive a copy for their own personal study. The geologist was leaning over the secretary's desk as Carter entered. She looked up. Her demeanor was crisp and alert, but her cool expression seemed to melt as she recognized him from the meeting.

"I'm sorry if I interrupted. I'm waiting for Major Van der Grif."

"We were just finishing anyway," the young woman remarked.

Aubrey gave the secretary some final instructions, then picked up her attaché case. She walked toward him.

"You are from the United States."

"Is that a question?"

She smiled.

"I am sorry. An awkward way of introducing oneself," she said, offering her hand. "I am Aubrey Erhardt."

"I know."

"And you are . . ."

"Nick Carter," he said, clasping her slender hand in his own. "It's a pleasure to meet you. I found your lecture fascinating."

She beamed.

"Thank you. It was nothing, really. My field is geology. A graduate student could have done the same."

"Do you mind if I don't believe that?"

"As you wish," she demurred.

They stared at one another. Their eyes locked. A ripple of excitement flowed through them both.

"Are all the women in South Africa as lovely and intelligent as you?"

"Mr. Carter, please!"

"Nick."

She looked at her shoes, then brought her eyes back to his.

"Is that what you Americans call a 'come on'?" she asked with a smile.

"I think it was," he admitted with a grin.

Again, he couldn't help but gaze at her. Deeply. As if to drink in her beauty. Her thick, blond hair was shoulder length, her complexion as flawless as any he'd ever seen.

"That's all right," she said, mirroring his fascination. "You may call me Aubrey."

"I hope to," he answered.

"I must be going."

She walked past him. His eyes followed.

"Mr. Carter—I mean, Nick," she said, "it occurs to me that you are a long way from home. Perhaps you'd like to join me for dinner this evening?"

It took him barely a fraction of a second to consider the offer.

"I'd be delighted."

"Esselen Avenue. The Central Towers. I shall be expecting you."

With that she left the office. He turned again to the desk where the secretary had been eavesdropping. Her eyes fell abruptly to her paperwork. Carter couldn't stop grinning.

THREE

Carter arrived at Aubrey Erhardt's apartment at eight o'clock, a chilled bottle of Johannesburg Riesling in hand. When she came to the door, he was delighted to see that she had abandoned the crisp, professional appearance of that afternoon for a more casual look: white slacks, a loose-fitting blouse, and sandals.

"Please come in," she said, holding open the door as he entered.

She followed a half step behind.

"A present," he offered, handing over the bottle.

"How nice. Care for a glass now?"

He nodded.

Aubrey brought him a corkscrew and a bucket of ice from the kitchen. Carter opened the bottle, then filled two glasses with the cool white wine. He proposed a toast as they sat together on the sofa.

"To blue diamonds," he said, touching the rim of his glass to hers. "As cool and mysterious as the blue eyes I'm staring into this evening."

Aubrey smiled. Her eyes sparkled as she sipped the wine from her glass. They seemed to emanate a magnetism as powerful as the most stunning of gems.

"Somehow the wine tastes better after a toast like that."

He chuckled. "I was hoping you'd feel that way." He took

another taste. "Are you expecting me to ask how a beautiful woman like you got involved in geology?"

"Why not? Everyone else does, so I'll tell you. My father was a geologist. We lived in Capetown near the Eastern Transvaal. When I was a child we would go hiking in the mountains there. It was a game we would play, identifying the different rock formations. I became fascinated with the field and eventually attended the University of Pretoria where I studied exploratory geology. Are you familiar with the field?"

Carter shook his head.

"It deals with locating reserves of precious stones and metal ores through studies related to the surrounding terrain. It's lucrative, as you might imagine, but also terribly interesting."

"And your father? He must be very proud of your success."

"My father is dead. He died years ago in an explosion."

"I'm so sorry. A mining accident?"

Aubrey looked down into her wine glass as if it were a bottomless abyss.

"No. A terrorist bomb. There are many of those these days. More than I care to talk about."

"I'm sorry," he said again.

She gulped the remainder of her wine.

"There's no need to be sorry. In my country we are immune to such tragedies. It is a way of life."

Carter couldn't help but take a step back mentally to assess the young woman before him. He guessed her to be in her mid-twenties, but there was an air about her that hinted at someone mature for her years. Perhaps, Carter mused, the instincts of survival played tricks with the chronology Americans took for granted. Could it be that living on the razor's edge of calamity caused everyone in South Africa to peer into the days and months ahead with the jaundiced eye of fatalism?

"Have you ever been married, Nick?" she asked suddenly.

Her directness amused him.

"No," he answered simply.

She smiled as he refilled their glasses.

"Neither have I."

"Is that something you look forward to?"

Her expression turned whimsical.

"I've thought about it. What girl hasn't? But that's not for me right now. I have my career, and there are other circumstances. I am certain that Major General Van der Grif has briefed you on the crisis my country is facing at the moment."

"You mean the find at Oranjemund?"

"I mean the entire premise of this nation, Nick! I know this is going to sound like government propaganda, but the Communists have been actively contributing to the fall of South Africa for decades. Today it has become an issue of international proportion, but we have been dealing with Soviet intervention on a daily basis. It's no secret that the Russians want the minerals that lie in the ground right here beneath our feet. Diamonds, of course! But also ninety percent of the free world's magnesium, eighty-five percent of its chromium, and sixty percent of its platinum. Shall I continue?"

These statistics were not unknown to Carter—those and a dozen others equally as impressive.

"No. You needn't go on. I also know that the Cape of Good Hope is the busiest sea lane in the world and that the majority of ships carrying oil to the United States pass through those waters."

Aubrey seized this additional information like a runner snatching his baton.

"That is precisely why our government is being underminded. If South Africa were to fall into the hands of Communists indebted to Moscow, the United States would suffer

31

an irrecoverable blow, both economic and military."

Carter raised his glass in agreement.

"I couldn't agree with you more," he said, taking another sip of wine.

What he couldn't tell her was that plans for a U.S. naval presence in Capetown were already in the works for the mid-1980s. Still, she seemed to sense that there was more to Nick Carter than met the eye.

She looked into her glass for a second, then looked up.

"They tell me you are a businessman, but I don't believe them."

"They tell me that you're a geologist. I don't believe that, either."

She was not easily rattled.

"Is it true?" she persisted. "Are you a businessman?"

"Ask me no questions and I'll tell you no lies."

She smiled at their chess match of wits. She touched her lips to the glass of crystal-clear wine.

"As you wish. Let's not ask questions. Let's just enjoy each other, even if it's only for tonight."

His mind stuck on the phrase "only for tonight." Again, that nuance of destiny. Considering the assignment he was about to embark upon, her words had the ring of philosophy.

Carter leaned over toward her. He kissed her gently on the lips. They fell open like the velvety petals of a rose as their tongues touched. She sank slowly back into the couch's soft cushions. Their faces were inches apart as he stared, submerged and spinning, into the blue depths of her eyes.

"Perhaps I should begin serving dinner," she whispered breathlessly.

"Are you hungry?"

"Not for food."

With that, Carter lifted her from the couch, then walked her into the bedroom. He placed her gently on the queen-size four-poster bed.

She slipped out of her blouse and slacks as he undressed. When he looked down again, Aubrey was nude and inviting.

He lay down beside her, then kissed her once more. They caressed like a man and woman famished for food or thirsting for water, and each was what the other so desperately needed.

Carter could hear her heart pounding, could feel the erotic forces growing within the two of them like volcanoes as he touched the intense heat between her legs.

"Take me, Nick! Please take me *now*," she begged.

He spread her long, perfect legs. She made a growl deep in her throat that switched midway to a sigh of satisfaction as he drove himself deep inside her. Her eyes floated dreamily to the ceiling. Her lips trembled, then opened wide. He pressed his mouth over hers. She bucked upward, then upward still more, until at last he could feel her body shudder with a convulsive explosion accompanied by a sharp cry.

Aubrey was asleep on his bare chest as he lay in silence contemplating their evening of lovemaking and the savage days that lay ahead. There were two top-secret cables that would go out first thing the next morning, he thought. The first concerned the use of satellite photos showing troop movements in Angola. The second concerned Aubrey Erhardt. It was not unreasonable for her to suspect that he worked for U.S. intelligence. On the other hand, it was equally as reasonable for him to suspect that after her studies at the university, Aubrey had taken a technical position with the SAI, South African Intelligence.

Carter eased himself out of bed, leaving his newfound lover in blissful slumber. He dressed quietly, then surveyed the bedroom. Folded on a chair beside the bed were the clothes that Aubrey had worn. He went through them. Nothing. He inspected her undergarments. Her panties. Nothing. Her bra. He examined the cups. His eyes stopped at something above the little bow between them. It was black and the size of a coffee bean. As he suspected, it was a microphone.

True, he had said nothing that would be useful to her or her employers, but nevertheless he felt it important to establish some ground rules. They were, assumedly, working on the same side in this affair, but he wanted Van der Grif, Coetzee, and the others to know that they weren't dealing with some amateur.

Carter walked into the living room where the bulk of their conversation had taken place. The tape recorder was undoubtedly voice operated. He held the little black button of a microphone to his lips, then counted to ten in a whisper. He listened for the tape to be set in motion.

"One, two," he whispered, then listened.

He walked toward the stereo.

"Three, four . . ." Again he listened.

Carter moved across the room to an end table. He opened the drawer.

"Five, six . . ."

He entered the dining room.

"Seven, eight . . ."

He heard a sound.

"Nine, ten . . ."

It was coming from under the table. He knelt down, then inspected its underside. There it was. The size of a pack of cigarettes. A recording device had been taped to the bottom of the table. He undid the adhesive tape, then rewound the miniature cassette.

"They tell me you are a businessman . . ."

Carter chuckled. *Leave it to a sexy woman, Souh African or otherwise*, he thought. He ejected the cassette, then pocketed it. He taped the recorder back in its original position. It was a minute later that a knock sounded at the door. He debated whether to answer it, then decided it might be interesting. Considering the late hour, it could be one of two possibilities: a lover, or an emergency that involved either of them and the Oranjemund mine. He decided to take the odds in any case.

When Carter opened the door he was not surprised to see a young man, smartly dressed and looking more as if it were 9:00 A.M. rather than 2:15.

"Mr. Carter?"

"Yes, I'm Carter."

The messenger smiled.

"I have a message from Major General Van der Grif. He said you might be here."

He took the missive from him as Aubrey entered the foyer. He tore open the envelope, then read: *Come to SAI headquarters immediately. A matter of some urgency. K. J. Van der Grif.*

When Carter looked up, the young SAI agent was still there. He reached into his pocket, produced a few bills, and pressed them into the young man's hand. The agent looked at the money, then back to Carter.

"Buy yourself a nightcap," Carter suggested as he closed the door.

He walked past Aubrey, into the living room.

"Van der Grif?"

"Yes," he answered absently. "He wants to see me right away."

"Does he say what it concerns?"

"No, but it's important. Can I catch a cab from here?"

"No. There are no cabs. Curfew begins for whites at midnight."

"How about a car? Can I borrow yours?"

"Yes," she said, nervously lighting a cigarette. "Let me get you the keys."

Carter followed her into the dining room where the faint aromas of cooking still hinted at the dinner they had missed hours before. Aubrey fished the car keys from her purse. She handed them to him.

"White Mercedes. It's in the lot out front."

He nodded.

"Thanks," he said, then started for the door. "I can't recall a more delicious dinner."

Aubrey smiled.

"Nick," she called after him, "if you think you seduced me, you are mistaken."

"Oh?"

"It was I who seduced you."

"I see. Then perhaps you'll let me take you to dinner tomorrow evening—I mean this evening. The Culembory at six? I'd like to try my luck again."

"Certainly," she said, her dazzling smile turning coy. "You will have my car, after all."

"That and some information I think you'll want to discuss."

Aubrey's expression was quizzical as he left the apartment. Moments later, after she'd checked the recorder, Carter was certain it would change to chagrin.

The interrogation rooms at SAI headquarters were stark. Each contained an electric fan, a metal table, and three folding chairs. Microphones and tape recorders were concealed within the concrete walls. A mirrored, one-way observation window was set into the steel door. It was through this that Van der Grif and Carter viewed the battered Kenyan.

"Who is he?"

"His name is Nathato Motlana. He is a SWAPO operative working in the Kenyan government."

"How was he captured?"

"Like most. Bragging to his chums in a Nairobi bistro."

"What has he done?"

The Major General gave Carter a long look, then waved to a guard sitting in a glass-paneled control booth. The electric lock clicked open with the push of a button.

"I think it best if you hear for yourself."

The head of South African national security entered the interrogation room, Carter following a short step behind. The odor was overpowering. A nauseating combination of dead cigarettes, sweat, and feces.

"Motlana!" Van der Grif greeted the black man with a smile. "It is good to see you in person. I have been watching films of you and your comrades for weeks."

The Kenyan's eyes narrowed with loathing. He sat bound at the ankles and wrists by U-shaped brackets. He spat on the

36

floor as the major general approached.

Van der Grif turned to one of the two other agents in the room.

"Have you offered our guest coffee?"

"I don't want no coffee," Motlana blurted.

The major general's eyes sparkled with anticipation behind his glasses.

"Very well, then. Let's talk, shall we?"

Carter watched as Nathato Motlana shook his head from side to side in obstinate refusal. He was in his early thirties. His eyes were sharp and nervous. The look of fear was like a maddened glint. The fact that he had been badly beaten was apparent; a large, bluish blotch covered the side of his face.

"Motlana, you will be reasonable. We are not here to hurt you as the police did." He touched the side of the Kenyan's face. "But what is that? A hit on the side of the head? Surely you realize that you are at our mercy here. We will do as we please with you until you talk, so why make this difficult?"

The Kenyan was listening. Van der Grif's logic was inescapable. Even as he sat pinioned to the chair, wires extended from beneath the table where electrodes had been clamped to the most private, most sensitive parts of his body.

The major general paced the floor before him.

"Now, this much is certain. You and another gentleman in the Kenyan government escorted a British smuggler named Neville Burdon from Keniatta Airport. Is that true?"

Motlana said nothing.

"I shall ask you a second time," Van der Grif threatened, a chilling sternness creeping into his voice. "You did escort Neville Burdon from Keniatta Airport five days ago, did you not?"

Again there was a silence that seemed to dangle in the air like a noose. Van der Grif nodded to his assistant. A green glow emanated from the "on" light of what interrogators labeled simply the "black box." The intensity of the electrical shock was low this time, but it was enough to cause Motlana to jerk upward in his chair like a grotesque marionette, tugged at either side of his upper and lower body by unseen wires and strings.

The major general assessed his subject.

"Need I ask again?"

The black man stared back wordlessly.

Van der Grif nodded once more to his assistant.

The current intensified. A low, wailing sound poured from Motlana's lips. It was foreign, as if it came not from the man, but from a thing. It was as if the very cells and molecules of his body were protesting, revolting at the pain inflicted upon them. A stench issued from beneath the table, the unmistakable odor of burnt human flesh.

The Kenyan's eyes were glazed with fear and agony. They raced unseeing from one corner of the room to the other, perhaps praying for some mystical passageway to suddenly erupt in the walls, giving him passage to freedom or even death.

"I talk," he whimpered, tears streaming down the sides of his face. "I talk! *I talk!*" he cried.

Van der Grif signaled his assistant. The current was lowered, then lowered again until the green light went dull. The electrodes were unclamped, and the Kenyan collapsed.

"Water!" Van der Grif demanded.

The second of his two assistants brought a pitcher of ice water to him. The major general threw it over his subject. Motlana's eyes rolled white in their sockets. His head raised slowly. He appeared now more like a frightened child than a man.

"Neville Burdon. You killed him, didn't you, Motlana?"

"No, no, no," he wailed. "Motlana no kill. I bring to Ithena and Russian."

"What Russian, Nathato?"

"Andrei. Advisor for Ithena."

Van der Grif shot Carter a sidelong glance. South Africans had been claiming direct military involvement on the part of the Soviets for years. *Perhaps this will convince the American*, he thought.

38

"And who else, Nathato? Who else was there with Burdon?"

"A Cuban. His name Ramirez. There was another," he said, "but Motlana swear he not know name!"

The Kenyan's eyes swam in his head as they darted to the black box, then back to his interrogator.

"And what did he bring them? What was it that Burdon brought to the Russian and the others?"

Motlana hesitated. Van der Grif looked to his assistant, about to give the signal to reconnect the clamps, but it was unnecessary.

"Diamond! Diamond! *He bring them diamond!*" Nathato Motlana screamed before he broke down crying, his chin bobbing up and down in semiconsciousness before coming to rest on his chest.

Van der Grif turned on his heel.

"He shall stand trial," he told his subordinates. "The charges are international espionage, smuggling, and murder. Unbind him. Put him in a comfortable cell. Mr. Carter," he said in the same breath, "we will discuss this?"

Carter walked with Van der Grif to his air-conditioned office on the second floor of the SAI building. He took a seat opposite the major general's desk. He lit a cigarette, one of his own with the initials N.C. embossed in gold on the filter.

"You were quite correct in the men you named as accomplices in this situation, Mr. Carter: Ithena, Andrei and Ramirez."

"So I gathered."

Van der Grif detected the note of cynicism in his voice. He cleared his throat as if to prove his discomfort.

"I apologize for what may appear to be a rather brutal means of interrogation. Unpleasant, but effective. We have no time for dallying, you must realize, and I thought you would want to hear the man's responses for yourself."

"I appreciate that."

Van der Grif lit a pipe. His expression was sober.

"There was one bit of information that you didn't hear that

you should know about.''

"Yes?"

"Vladimir Andrei knows you're here, Mr. Carter. Motlana made a point of that as if to prove we are not the only
ones capable of gathering intelligence. The Russian is aware
that an American 'advisor' has been sent to South Africa for
the express purpose of thwarting an invasion of Namibia.''

Andrei. Van der Grif didn't need to elaborate. Anyone
familiar with the politics of Africa over the past decade knew
of Vladimir Andrei, the KGB's foremost operative on the
continent. Ruthless and cunning, he had been considered
something of a prodigy upon his arrival in Africa during the
early seventies, but by now that raw talent had been honed to
a precision that left him far and away the best the Soviets had
to offer. A formidable opponent, Carter mused in silence.
Carter knew of Andrei. Now Andrei knew of Carter.

"Thanks. It's always an advantage to be aware of what the
opposition knows. I'll be mindful of it.''

He reached into his jacket pocket.

"Yesterday I mentioned some cables I'd like sent
stateside. Here they are. I'd appreciate it if you got them off
as soon as possible.''

Van der Grif examined them perfunctorily.

"But there are five,'' he protested. "Surely you're not
using decoys!''

Carter smiled wryly as the major general studied them
further.

"And they are scrambled! Mr. Carter, need I remind you
that we are working together in this undertaking?''

"No,'' Carter retorted, reaching into his pants pocket.
"That's one reason I was surprised to discover this in Aubrey
Erhardt's apartment this morning.''

Carter tossed the miniature cassette on the desk as he rose.

"I'll be expecting responses by tomorrow afternoon. Five
responses. All of them scrambled. Good day, Major Van der
Grif.''

The head of South African national security made no

attempt to respond. Instead, he placed his hand over the tiny tape recording, then wrapped his fingers around it tightly.

"Good day, Mr. Carter," he uttered softly as the door to his office closed behind the American agent.

FOUR

The Czech-made twin-engine prop plane warmed up at an unnamed landing strip outside the town of Xangongo, Angola. Inside the craft, six SWAPO guerrillas inspected their supplies and munitions in preparation for the most daring mission their organization had ever undertaken. Each of the two teams studied the maps of their targets. The first was the Oranjemund mine. The second, the hydroelectric generating station in Johannesburg. Both had been chosen by the military advisors assigned to aid SWAPO for maximum tactical and psychological effect. Strategically, any delay in mining the boron-coated diamonds would buy time for the Soviets. Psychologically, there was no more vicious assault to the psyche of the South Africans than to destroy the very foundation of their presumed superiority over the rest of Africa: technology. This logic, the guerrillas did not attempt to comprehend. Theirs was a far more basic understanding. If they failed, they would die. If they succeeded, they would also die, but the South-West African People's Organization would be that much closer to tearing loose from the yoke of white, South African domination.

The Ocesky Air King headed down the runway. It was just past midnight. The African sky was dark and overcast, a perfect sky to camouflage the border crossing of the small craft. The town of Xangongo was just fifty miles inside the

43

Angolan border, and it took only a matter of minutes before the SWAPO soldiers found themselves passing over the Cunene River, which separated their current sanctuary from Namibia. They crossed it at treetop level to avoid radar detection. Still, the six soldiers and one pilot watched the ground below as a border guard searched the black night, then took aim with his rifle. He fired three shots without effect. Alerted by the shots, several of his countrymen joined in the assault as the pilot throttled his engines, then raced away into the darkness.

"Any damage?" one of the guerrillas called forward in a Venda dialect.

The pilot, who was from the Sotho tribe, did not understand.

"Go to hell!" he shouted back, purposely using his native tongue, one of twenty-seven that existed in the region. "You worry about yourself! I worry about the plane!"

No one in the back understood or cared to, since they, like most members of SWAPO, belonged to the Venda tribe, and each tribe considered the other hopelessly primitive.

The guerrilla simply shrugged to the others.

"What is a Sotho doing here anyway?" he asked rhetorically. The five black men just shook their heads, then laughed.

The first team was getting edgy. Even though their mission was less dangerous than that of their counterparts, they would be parachuting into the heart of Oranjemund. De Beers Consolidated Diamond Mines had fenced off this barren slice of Namibia from the rest of the world, calling it Sperrgebeit—the forbidden territory. It was their domain, a hellish strip of terrain where a city had literally been constructed around the mining site. Security was very tight. High, double-barbed, electrified fences surrounded the rambling pit where diamonds were excavated. Workers were X-rayed and strip searched on a daily basis. Guards armed with high-powered weapons and the most sophisticated surveillance equipment known to modern science were used along each step of the hunt for diamonds. From the processing area, where crushed rocks passed through fluoroscopes and diamonds were separated from stones of similar density, to the vault at De Beers's central office, where the uncut gems were classified on the basis of size, color, clarity, and weight, few activities passed unobserved by Oranjemund's crack security forces. But these measures were of no concern to the three guerrillas who sat nervously awaiting the go-ahead. The security at Oranjemund was designed to prevent the illegal flow of diamonds from the complex. SWAPO's aim had nothing to do with that; it had to do with sabotage, a far easier task considering the mine's isolated location.

The pilot had brought the plane to an altitude of five thousand feet. He began a slow, steady descent. His eyes fell upon the massive bright spot below. This was Koingnaas, the series of alluvial mines where the crucial diamonds had been discovered. Floodlights lit the areas behind three parallel dikes that prevented the waters of the mighty Atlantic from rushing into the huge pit to reclaim the land that was rightfully hers.

This is it, the pilot reflected. The danger was now as tangible as the sweat that covered the palms of his hands. Target number one lay just a few short miles southwest and thirty-five hundred feet below.

"You three monkeys!" the pilot called in Sotho. "Get ready to jump!"

It required no understanding of the dialect for the three SWAPO guerrillas to respond. They had been waiting for just such a directive for weeks. Trained by a cadre of Cuban commandos under the direction of Carlos Ramirez, they represented the elite of what was at best an ill-trained but highly motivated army.

They stood, an odd mixture of fear and duty welling within their chests. No, they wouldn't be returning, they thought, looking down upon the ultramodern mining site. More than a complex, it was a way of life they were attacking, the sophistication of a progressive technology whose radar and weapons and systems of surveillance would not allow them to survive. The South African government would hunt down these invaders with a vengeance.

The pilot took the plane down an additional thousand feet. His engines idled as he coasted just above the water. The sea was calm. The reflection of searchlights, aimed toward the land, was visible on the shimmering ocean.

"Now!" the pilot ordered in a loud rasp. "Jump now!"

The three men leaped from the plane on command. Their pea-green parachutes opened at fifteen hundred feet. They drifted together, landing in the water at staggered intervals. The group leader cut loose the cords that attached him to the sagging nylon sheet. His two subordinates did the same.

Each of the men was equipped with an inflatable life raft. Again, the group leader was the first to react. He pierced the gas cartridge. The raft grew large as he threw one leg over it, and the others swam toward him. They discarded their own flat backup rafts, which promptly sank into the depths of the ocean.

"Come on!" he ordered.

His subordinates each took paddles. They dug into the black water and traveled toward the first of the three massive dikes that protected the below-sea-level operation at Oranjemund.

Overhead, the three guerrillas could hear the sound of the plane's engines as the Sotho pilot accelerated on the way to the second target deep in the heart of South Africa: the hydroelectric generating station in Johannesburg.

Sirens screamed like wounded animals in the night as Nick Carter and Aubrey Erhardt made their way up the stairs to Carter's room at the Culembory Hotel. Though there was a midnight curfew, the hotel bar stayed open into the early morning hours for guests, and they had made the best of their time together. Carter had received word back from the Pentagon regarding access to satellite photos of the Angolan military buildup, and it was affirmative. And he had learned the truth about Aubrey: pages of information that relieved him on the one hand but filled him with grave misgivings on the other.

"What do you suppose is going on out there?" Carter asked.

"It must be a bombing. Maybe several. I don't think I've ever heard so many sirens at once."

"Sounds like all hell's broken loose. Could it be SWAPO?"

"Nick, it's almost certainly SWAPO. That's how bad it has gotten."

When they arrived at the third-floor landing, Carter could sense an odor in the air. It was perspiration. He hesitated for a moment.

Aubrey looked to him curiously. "What is it, Nick?"

He didn't answer, unable to since it was only a perception as elusive as a creaking step in the early morning or a glint in the eye of a supposed friend who had altered allegiance.

The hallway was lit, though dimly. It was in the shape of an L, the staircase running up from its center.

Carter walked silently down the corridor leading to his room. The possibility of danger had yet to dawn on Aubrey as she followed behind him in silence. It must have registered when he reached for his holster and drew out his 9mm Luger, affectionately called Wilhelmina.

"What . . . ?" Aubrey began.

He turned and placed the tip of his index finger to her lips.

I don't know, his eyes answered. *I just don't know for certain.*

The door to his room was closed. The lights were out as he had left them. He checked the lock to see if it had been tampered with; it hadn't been touched. But waves of intuition warned him that something was wrong.

Carter stood to the side of the door, then put his ear to the wood. Inside, he could hear the whispered command of one man to another. He was right. Perhaps it had been Van der Grif's warning that Andrei knew of his presence in South

Africa, or the information he'd received with regard to Aubrey's true identity, but something had alerted him. His hunch was on target. The tentacles of the Soviet KGB had extended into South Africa. Indeed, they had extended into his very room and were waiting there to put an end to his life.

"Stay here," he whispered to Aubrey. "And whatever happens, don't make a sound."

She nodded woodenly. Her face was white.

Carter trotted to the end of the hallway where a casement window faced Schaumberg Avenue. A narrow ledge ran around the hotel, punctuated by balconies that protruded from each of the streetside rooms. Covered with stucco and enclosed with fancy wrought-iron railings, they had been long neglected and seemed incapable of supporting much more than a few potted plants. Still, if he used the ledge as a catwalk leading to the balcony outside his room, there was an excellent chance he'd be able to catch his would-be assassins unawares.

Carter opened the window, studying the balcony and the narrow shelf that ran alongside it. Cautiously, he stepped out onto the narrow ledge, edging his way along the building's north side. He leaned his weight against the wall, going foot over foot, one step at a time. He paced his breathing so that it coincided with his gait. Step, breath, step, breath, until he could reach out to grab the iron railing of the next terrace. He took hold of it, then climbed over. The next few yards would be a snap, he thought, pausing to listen for sounds from the room. Nothing. He strode across the balcony, startled to feel the give in the bolts that riveted it to the building. The platform leaned at a twenty-degree angle with his weight as he stepped from it onto the ledge once more. He took a deep breath, then began the short half-steps that made every yard of distance seem like a mile.

Carter moved slowly but efficiently, careful not to get overconfident. To rouse a sleeping guest would result in his being arrested or shot outright. He kept reminding himself of this as if to tame an overwhelming impulse to hurry along recklessly. He hugged the side of the building, palms pressed against it as he crept nearer and nearer to the next balcony. He stood back, straight and tense, sidling the wall. Below him and across the street stood a small restaurant, two storefronts, and a movie theater. *Thank God there's no one down there*, he thought, taking note of his exposed position. The second balcony was within reach. He stopped and was about to take hold of the railing, when he heard the tapping sound of high heels on the pavement below. *Damn!* he cursed, freezing in his tracks. His breathing stopped. The sound of his pounding heart seemed audible as he glanced downward and caught a glimpse of a South African soldier and a prostitute.

"Where have you been?" the man asked drunkenly.

"You think you own me?" she shot back. "You ain't the only man in Johannesburg, you know."

The soldier must have grabbed her, because Carter could hear her grunt as he spoke in a throaty whisper.

"Look! See what I brought you? You like this, don't you?"

"Where did you get that?"

"That is for me to know, but if you want the cocaine, it comes with a price."

Carter listened, mesmerized, as she broke away from the soldier's grip.

"You are a pig!" she hissed.

"But you love me, don't you?"

There was a lull in their conversation as she considered his offer.

The next sound Carter heard was that of high heels tapping on the pavement once more. The soldier laughed. His stumbling footsteps sounded behind hers as they entered the Culembory Hotel together.

Carter closed his eyes solemnly. He ran his hand through his hair. It was wet with perspiration. He extended his arm tentatively, as much a feeler as an appendage, then grabbed the iron rail of the second balcony. He leaned over it, listening for sounds from inside the room before him. He peered

49

inside, barely able to distinguish the silhouette of a figure in bed as it turned over, snoring. Carter leaped onto the balcony. He hurried across it, mounted the ledge, then stopped. Ten steps away stood the terrace leading to his own room.

Carter took Wilhelmina from her holster and attached a silencer. Any hesitancy that might have tempered his actions earlier had long since disappeared as he took the few remaining steps that separated him from his quarry. He was all professional now, and trained instinct—not prudence—was his master. Since Soviet hit men usually worked in teams of two, the odds of taking them both alive were slim. Even with the drop on them, Carter was pretty sure one or the other would fire. Still, he would attempt to keep this as clean as possible. These men would be valuable, if only for their general knowledge concerning KGB operations on the continent. Carter's expression grew taut as he came upon the edge of the balcony leading to his darkened room.

He stood stock-still. Not a sound emanated from within the room. Carter reached for the iron railing. It felt cold and forbidding. He eased himself over the top by degrees. His body tensed as he placed one foot on the terrace, shifting his weight from the ledge. A tingling sensation of panic cut through him in an instant. The balcony was breaking away from its moorings!

Carter's eyes shot to the window as he stood half on and half off the ledge. He prayed that the men inside hadn't heard him and that the balcony would support him for the few seconds it would take to get off three or four rounds. His temples ached, the blood in his head throbbing. His eyes lifted to the window again. If the Soviets had heard anything, they hadn't reacted. Yet.

He steeled his jangled nerves. Inch by inch, pound by pound, he lowered himself onto the balcony. Below him he could hear the sound of plaster and cement as it sprinkled down to the pavement. He visualized the room's layout before making his move: a desk, a bureau with mirror, and a bed that hugged the north wall. *Now!* his mind said. He threw

50

his full weight down onto the balcony. He fired. One, two, three shots crashed through the window. He heard the cry of a man. It was the last sound he heard before tumbling down to the deadly whistle of return fire. Carter had no time to react as he plunged the ten feet to the floor below. Wilhelmina, frozen in his right hand, fired randomly as he slammed, shoulder first, onto the floor of the terrace. He looked up. Above him, the third-floor balcony dangled precariously from its one remaining support.

Once back in the room, Carter examined the body of one of the two assailants he'd fired upon. He had never seen him before, but he appeared to be of Slavic descent, probably Russian. He had taken two bullets just before the balcony gave way. He hadn't bled much, and to Carter he seemed more asleep than dead. The corpse's partner had vanished.

Aubrey entered the room slowly. Her steps were hesitant as she approached Carter.

"Is he . . . ?"

"Yes," Carter answered. "Quite dead."

"But why? What reason could they have for wanting to kill you?"

"Me? Maybe me. But it's just as likely they were after you. I got a cable from my people in the States today. It gave me a rundown on the work your father had been engaged in prior to his death."

"I don't know what you're talking about."

"I think you do. Your father was one of the world's foremost experts on laser beam technology. The experiments he had been conducting promised to put South Africa ten years ahead of both the United States and Russia. He's dead now. That leaves just you, Aubrey, and thanks to his work you are one of the most influential laser researchers in the world today. My guess is that the Soviets want you badly. Preferably alive, so they can use you. If not that, then dead—so the United States can't."

"Did you expect me to tell you that over cocktails, Nick? I know you work for the CIA, or did you discover how to detect hidden microphones at Harvard Business School?''

"You're right. I'm no businessman, but all of that is unimportant. What is important is that you stay protected. Your knowledge of the blue diamonds is as vital to the interests of both our countries as the stones themselves. Now close that door. I have to make a phone call."

Aubrey craned her head around the doorway, checking for the police who were certain to be on their way because of the shots. She closed the door as Carter dialed Van der Grif's home number.

It took several rings for the major general to answer. Carter poured himself a few fingers of scotch in the interim.

"Yes? What is it?"

"It's Carter," he answered, taking a long swig from the glass. "I'm afraid I have a body to dispose of."

"You what??"

"A body. Russian, I think. I'm with Aubrey. I can't say which of us they were after, but I got to him first."

"Have the police arrived yet?"

"No."

"Do you think they've been alerted?"

Carter looked around the room. The window had been shot out, the balcony had collapsed, and a body lay before him.

"I'd say so," he answered.

"Don't say anything until I get there. Just stay where you are. I'll see what I can do."

"Thanks. I'll be waiting," he retorted, hanging up the receiver.

He turned to Aubrey. Her eyes were wide with fright.

"What did he say?"

"He said not to worry, that he would take care of everything. I believe him."

Aubrey sat down on the edge of the bed, drained.

"And one other thing," Carter added.

Her head bobbed up. "Yes?"

"From now on you'll be staying with me."

FIVE

The ambulance arrived at the hotel several moments before
Van der Grif. Though the attendants were dressed in the
uniform of city hospital workers, it was apparent that they
were SAI people from their demeanor and the fact that they
asked no questions. When Aubrey introduced herself to explain what had happened, the detectives who accompanied
them stated simply, "We know who you are."

Within minutes, the corpse was zipped into a plastic body
bag, and carried to the waiting ambulance. The vehicle sped
off without a siren, leaving Aubrey wondering if the entire
episode had really happened.

"They weren't from the city hospital, were they?" she
asked.

Carter shook his head.

"And the detectives. They weren't detectives either, were
they?"

Again he shook his head.

Aubrey took a moment to let the realization of what
actually happened run through her mind.

"What *is* real, Nick?"

Carter smiled.

"You're real. I'm real. I also believe that the cause we're
fighting for in South Africa is real. The rest is just trim-
ming." He winked. "Welcome to the world of espionage,

Aubrey. You've opened the door. I'm afraid there's no turning back now."

"But I don't want any part of this!" she sputtered. "I've never even seen a dead person before tonight!"

Carter poured himself another three fingers of scotch. He offered Aubrey the same. She accepted with a nod.

"Here's hoping you never see another," he said, throwing back the drink. "But my guess is, you will."

A knock sounded at the door. Carter opened it. From behind his gold-rimmed glasses, Van der Grif stared at him through bloodshot eyes.

"The ambulance was here? There was no trouble?"

"No. None."

"The girl?" He turned to Aubrey. "Are you all right?"

Despite a quivering chin, she said that she was.

Carter's eyes rose to meet Van der Grif's.

"Did you get an ID on the body?"

"His passport has him as Soren Nabokov. A Russian. Did you know him?"

"I know the name," Carter answered. "Worked for the KGB. He was Vladimir Andrei's right-hand man, or so they say."

"Well, we'll be running a full check of fingerprints and dental records to confirm the identity. Unfortunately, it looks as if his comrade has eluded our security net . . ."

Van der Grif continued talking, but Carter's mind was elsewhere. Nabokov had been one of the KGB's top agents. The Killmaster had never met him, but the Russian's presence let Carter know that the Kremlin was playing hardball.

The sound of Van der Grif's voice jarred him from his thoughts.

"You will have to excuse my appearance, but it has been an extremely trying evening. You've undoubtedly been hearing the sirens."

"We have. What happened?"

"Bombings. The worst we've ever experienced. Two targets: the hydroelectric generating station in Johannesburg and the mining site at Oranjemund."

"How did they do it?"

"Plastic explosives. Customs officials stopped a crate at Jan Smuts Airport loaded with nitroglycerin and cellulose nitrate. They also found surface-to-air missiles. It seems there was a plot afoot to down an SAA commercial airliner!"

"How's the mine?"

"Work has been stopped indefinitely. It's hopelessly flooded."

"Flooded? I don't follow."

"The mine at Oranjemund is alluvial. That is, below sea level. De Beers had to reclaim the land by building a series of dikes to hold back the water. It was these dikes the SWAPO soldiers managed to damage. I'm told a wall of water thirty feet high rushed into the pit. Nearly one hundred miners are drowned or missing."

His expression conveyed the gravity of the situation. If the mining operation could be sabotaged once, what about a second and even a third time? The question that arose was a simple one: if sabotage was now a constant threat, would they ever be able to mine the boron-coated diamonds successfully?

"Have they caught anyone?"

"Three blacks were shot dead outside of Johannesburg. In theory, that's a catastrophe because, like Nabokov, we wanted them for questioning. Practically speaking, it doesn't mean a damned thing. We know what we're up against. We even know who we're up against. The question is, how do we stop them?"

The answer was obvious, Carter thought. The SWAPO guerrillas had to be routed from Angola.

Aubrey stood. She walked slowly toward the men.

"Has anyone from the CDM surveyed the damage?"

"I'm certain they have by now. The flood was instantaneous. I would suspect salvage operations are underway at this very moment."

"Then I should be there," she volunteered. "Even with the main pit flooded, there is a strong possibility mining can continue elsewhere."

She had their attention.

"You see, in alluvial mining there is no one kimberlite vein from which the diamonds are drawn. Instead, they come from veins miles away that were eroded by water eons ago. From there, they were carried downstream or to an ocean bed like Oranjemund. In Sierra Leone, the diamonds from three small veins are dispersed in an area more than fifty miles from their source. Oranjemund should be no different."

"Would you be willing to fly with me to the mining site to discuss this with our engineers?" asked Van der Grif.

"You mean now—this morning?"

"I mean immediately."

Aubrey looked to Carter.

"Nick, will you join us?"

"I was hoping you'd ask."

The three left Pretoria about two hours later in a twin-engine Beechcraft. The course they took was to the northwest. It was apparent after an hour that they were leaving the more developed terrain of South Africa for the barren plains beyond the Namibian border. Signs of habitation were nonexistent until the seemingly endless desert below was punctuated by a cluster of low, flat buildings. This was the mine complex. Beyond it was the Orange River. Long and winding, it was from this that the name Oranjemund derived. Meaning literally "orange mouth," it was this water source that millions of years ago, had eroded the kimberlite veins, carrying the precious stones it concealed miles away to the alluvial pit where they were now mined. Stretching out westward, Carter could discern the three huge dikes that hours ago had restrained the mighty Atlantic. Now the huge pit before the third dike was filled like an enormous pool as rescue parties scurried in small marine craft to retrieve the floating bodies of laborers caught unawares by the onrushing wall of water. Debris bobbed in the pit below, lit by piercing swaths of light directed from batteries of searchlights positioned above the mine.

"They probably never knew what hit them," Carter commented as the plane circled the disaster area.

"Hmmm," said Van der Grif absently. "I was also just thinking about those men."

"What about them?" Aubrey asked gently.

"About the families of the men and how varied their backgrounds must have been. Ovambo tribesmen, Brits, Afrikaaners—over a hundred dead at last count. I was just thinking how strange for them all to die together in that huge, water-filled crater. No apartheid. No class distinction. Nothing more complicated than the cold reality of death."

No one said a word after that. Privately, Carter was surprised to see the compassion Van der Grif held for those who had died. He genuinely mourned them. There was a sense of humanity to the man.

The Beechcraft landed on a short paved runway on the Namibian side of the Orange River. Beside it was a long, flat concrete structure known as the clearing terminal. Here, all visitors were searched and their clothes inspected before entering or leaving the mining complex. This represented the only on-land entrance to the mine. Beyond its tall electrified fences was not only the excavation, but the town of Oranjemund itself, complete with grocery stores, movie theaters, and recreational facilities. Such was the isolation that no cars, mobile equipment, or even electrical appliances would ever move beyond the southern side of the complex gates.

Aubrey, Van der Grif, and Carter submitted to the search. They left their valuables behind, then donned the white coveralls and hard hat that each of the town's eight thousand inhabitants were expected to wear when entering the mine. A beige Mercedes was waiting once they'd passed through the clearing terminal. An engineer named Kallie Bloem drove them from the outside gates through the neat town, then toward the river mouth where the salvage operation continued.

A second set of gates greeted them. Armed guards stood watching at either side as closed circuit video cameras scanned the length and breadth of the Mercedes. Bloem handed them the plastic electromagnetic cards that carried their identification numbers. The numbers were routinely run through a computer that contained application information submitted by the SAI. The gates opened with a mechanized hum. Their car proceeded along a desert road that ran approximately five miles to the south of the Orange River. From there they drove up toward the rim of the mining pit. They stopped some one hundred yards from the edge, then hiked the remaining distance on foot. Above them, emergency helicopters hovered, lifting both men and equipment from the flooded area.

"We're at something of a disadvantage as far as rescue operations here because of security," Kallie Bloem explained. "We can't allow just anyone in, which you can understand, but people are damned greedy when it comes to diamonds, and even our own people will make a go for it if they see the opportunity."

The four of them made their way up the steep incline. The major general elaborated.

"Kallie is referring to a roundup we had only this morning after the explosion. Twenty-three Ovambos were arrested by security in an attempt to smuggle diamonds. The irony of it is that they were using them to help finance SWAPO."

He said nothing more. He didn't have to. The unspoken conclusion was that the Republic of South Africa had enemies everywhere, on the borders that surrounded it and even internally among those its technology supported.

It was only after they'd reached the outer edge of the mine that the full extent of the rescue operation could be appreciated. The four of them stood like aliens viewing some foreign civilization from the edge of the abyss. The pit itself stretched better than a half mile in length and a quarter mile across, and was some one hundred feet below sea level at its deepest point. Above it, helicopters plucked survivors from the water. Below, hundreds of hydraulic pumps labored feverishly, spewing water beyond the third dike, which was presently being fortified by armies of bulldozers that heaped sand along its towering bank.

"Do you have any idea how long mining operations will be suspended?" Aubrey asked Bloem.

Kallie Bloem scratched his long sideburns.

"Indefinitely." He looked at her apologetically. "I'm sorry, miss, but that's the best I can do. I've never seen anything this bad, so I have nothing to go by."

"Have core samples been taken along the river bed?"

"I doubt it. Down here, the mine runs just half a mile north. We've stuck to no particular pattern, because the diamonds aren't evenly distributed. We find an area that's rich, then stick to it. So far, that's been south, out farther into the Atlantic."

Aubrey nodded.

"I'd be willing to bet the Orange River has changed course dozens of times during the past millennia. If that's the case," she continued as if thinking out loud, "the same type of boron-coated diamonds should be strewn all along those dry beds. Perhaps not in the same quantities, but there nevertheless."

She broke from her train of thought abruptly.

"Gentlemen, it's my opinion that if we trace the flow of the Orange River back far enough, we will discover dry, ancient terraces that may be diamond-bearing. If that much is true, there is a distinct possibility that the type eleven-B stones are among them and can be mined in the very near future at an above-ground location."

Van der Grif's interest was piqued.

"Bloem, can that be done?"

"By all means! We take core samples every day. Of course, I'll need a go-ahead from headquarters . . ."

"You will have it. After today, I believe the military will be having a lot more to say about the operations here at Oranjemund, starting with security. I intend to petition the prime minister personally about such authority.''

Kallie Bloem's countenance brightened despite the situation.

"Miss Erhardt, do you think you could indicate on a map exactly where those terraces might be?''

"It will take a little research, some geological study, and an examination of earth samples, but I could give you a good idea within a day or two.''

"Excellent!'' concluded the major general. "Then it's decided; plans for a secondary mine will be put into effect immediately. Bloem, I promise you clearance from the head office by tomorrow morning.''

The discussion ended on an optimistic note, but it had a hollow ring. The reality of the death and devastation below was overwhelming. It had become apparent to Carter during even this short exposure that unless SWAPO's foreign braintrust were neutralized, the terrorists would bring South Africa to her knees in a matter of months. True, Aubrey's theory regarding a secondary stratum of diamond deposits might yield a new mine, but would that one be any less vulnerable to sabotage? *Not when the very workers who dig the diamonds are SWAPO operatives*, he thought.

"Major, may I see you for a moment? Alone?''

Van der Grif excused himself. Together they drifted out of earshot.

"I was going to wait to tell you this, but under the circumstances I thought you could use some good news. Your government has been granted access to U.S. satellite intelligence on Angola. The photos will be transmitted on a daily basis and more frequently if it becomes necessary. It should help our situation considerably.''

"God knows we need it,'' he muttered through thin, drawn lips. "They've never hit us like this before, Nick. Not on our home turf. They not only penetrated De Beers security to cripple the mining operation, but they found their way to our doorstep to damage the hydroelectric station in Johannesburg. The consequences of such successes are more far-reaching than you can imagine.''

"How so?''

"If SWAPO can get to Johannesburg, they can get any-where. There will be a panic here in South Africa the likes of which we have never seen. A public outcry for a full-scale invasion of Angola has already been voiced, but right-wing activists will be calling for even tighter security. That means more curfews, more arrests, and even harsher restrictions on blacks. Need I go further?''

"Internal unrest is the last thing South Africa needs at this point,'' Carter agreed. "We have to move and move fast. Any word from the surveillance contingent you sent over the border last week?''

"Nothing. Not even indirect contact through the handful of in-place agents we still have operating in Luanda.''

"You think they were captured?''

"Tortured then executed, most likely. If that's the case, we lost much more than we gained. They may now realize how little we know about what the Soviets are planning.''

Carter considered the bleak prospects that their current situation afforded.

"Any idea how the U.N. would react to a simple assault into Angola after this? Couldn't these bombings be used as justification for a first strike at SWAPO and its backers?''

"Our credibility in the United Nations is nonexistent. South Africa's great sin is that it does not live by majority rule. It is a trespass for which we will never be forgiven, but I ask you: what African country should we emulate as a model of majority rule? Tanzania, one of the world's twenty-five poorest nations? Starving Chad? Inflation-ravaged Nigeria? Cuban-occupied Angola? Africa is the poorest and most backward continent on earth. It has experienced fifty coups d'état since 1960.'' He guffawed. "An invasion into Angola now would be the final nail in our coffin. The worldwide economic sanctions under debate would be put into effect within forty-eight hours of such an assault.''

"And that's the only reason?''

Van der Grif reached for his glasses. He cleaned them with a practiced consideration.

"No. That is not the only reason. There is another circumstance that concerns me and that is that the Soviets seem almost to be baiting us into an attack. It leads me to believe they think they can win and that the first series of satellite photos will reveal that munitions have been pouring into Angola through Moçâmedes for months.''

His logic had Carter recalling his last briefing with David Hawk in Washington. Hawk had said something then that now stuck like a fishhook in the back of Carter's brain: the Soviets would risk World War III over those diamonds, his boss had predicted. Given the scenario of a first strike by South African forces, Carter was convinced that the Russians would come to Angola's defense and attempt to take Namibia on SWAPO's behalf. He also realized now why permission for use of top-secret U.S. satellite photos was so easily granted: the Pentagon was concerned that the Soviets had South Africa checkmated before they'd even gotten involved.

Carter lit a cigarette.

"Those mercenaries,'' he said at last. "The ones this whole controversy started over—where are they now?''

"Some are in prison here awaiting trial. The others just seem to drift around the continent waiting for work. They are seldom disappointed. Someone is always willing to put them to use somewhere in Africa.''

"Could you get a group together? No more than six. But I want the best. Total professionals. No criminal records. Men who were never officially connected to previous incursions across the border.''

"That shouldn't be too difficult. We have our lists, you know.''

Carter nodded.

"I'd like to go over those lists, then I'll decide who'll be coming with me."

"With you?"

"It's time we made our move, Karl. The key to this is putting Andrei, Ramirez, and Ithena out of the picture. Without that braintrust, SWAPO will be left with a lot of military hardware and no plan to use it."

SIX

The British sailor was obviously thirsty as he swaggered
up to the entrance of Mobutu's in Port Nolloth, Namibia. He
was burly and feisty, long prepared for his two-day layover in
Namibia on the way to Oman. His eyes took in the unlit neon
sign that read Mobutu's Old London Pub. A tired smile
passed over his leathery face at the sight of the landmark
familiar to him from six previous hauls. His pace quickened
as he approached the entrance. He was curious but not surprised to see three South African military personnel at the
pub's entrance. He stepped up to the doorway between them.
Two G3 rifles blocked his path.

"Hey, mates, what's this all about?"

"Mobutu's is closed for the night," the largest of the three
soldiers replied.

"Closed? It bloody well better not be closed! I walked all
the way from the docks to get here!"

"Go to Sam's," the second soldier suggested. "That pub
is open tonight."

"But the lights is on inside!" the British sailor persisted,
pushing his way forward.

Again he was stopped. This time physically.

The strapping Afrikaaner corporal lost his patience. He
held his rifle beneath the sailor's chin.

"Don't you understand English, buddy? The pub is closed!"

The stunned sailor swallowed hard as he took three steps backward. Behind him and to his right and left stood no fewer than seven armed South African militiamen.

"It's a bloody battalion you blokes got here," he muttered almost to himself. "I—I must have come to the wrong place. Sorry, mates," he stammered as he turned sideways, then ran from the bar.

Inside Mobutu's, seated at a long narrow table in a back room, were eight men including Karl Van der Grif and Nick Carter. The other six were an assortment of Rhodesian, New Zealand, American, and Portuguese mercenaries, the disheveled remnants of the band of soldiers for hire who had been killed, captured, or arrested after South Africa's most recent raid into Angola. It was a motley crew. Their ad hoc leader, a white Rhodesian name Eric "Mad Dog" Shea, sat with his elbows on the table, quietly sipping a mug of Manica beer. Around him were seated "Doc" Barnes, a black American demolitions expert, Anthony "One Shot" Ward, who claimed mortars as his specialty, Enrico Chargas, a Portuguese native of Angola, and two New Zealanders, Peter Wesson and Ian Hardy, each trained to the gills in the use of small weapons and hand-to-hand combat.

Carter stood before the group, a few maps taped to a blackboard behind him. The men seemed more like a band of beery athletes than mercenaries as each stared ahead, their expressions as faithless as any he'd ever seen. To them, this was just another job, nothing more and nothing less.

"You six men were invited here because you're the best at what you do. You've worked before for the interests I'm representing. They pay well and they pay on time. If you decide to accept the mission, the salary will be paid in Krugerrands—gold—in the amount of a thousand dollars American per day. If our venture is successful, you'll each be receiving an additional five grand in bonus money."

He scanned the six faces before him. Reaction was

nonexistent despite the generous offer.

"Okay," growled Shea, sipping from his mug of beer. "What do we do to earn this king's ransom?"

Carter didn't blink.

"Kill or capture three men. All highly protected. All entrenched in a military compound one hundred miles inside Angola."

Shea shrugged and finished his Manica. Foam ran down his unshaven chin. He wiped it away with the sleeve of his shirt.

"Commies?"

Carter nodded.

"What kind of weapons do we have?"

"You name it. We're not cutting any corners. We can't afford to."

"Explosives," said Doc Barnes as if it were the only word in his vocabulary. "How 'bout them?"

"Any kind you want, provided they can be carried. We're going into the bush. Part of the way by jeep. The rest on foot."

He grunted. Carter assumed it was his way of expressing approval.

"You said military compound. I ain't takin' on no FAPLA headquarters with five men," Ward complained. "Even with explosives."

His large, rheumy eyes widened.

"And another thing. I want to know who we're workin' for now, up front. If it's the South African government, say so. We've all got our reputations. A talkin' mercenary is worth less than a pregnant whore. We all know that. So let's have it. I ain't workin' for some half-assed U.S. corporation that's gonna pull out on us once the road gets a little rocky."

Carter cast a cool stare in Van der Grif's direction. Dressed in civilian clothes, he looked different, more civilized than the rest of them. The spectator who could view the goings-on around him, sigh with disappointment if the game had not gone his way, then walk away from it all.

"Tell them," the major general retorted bluntly.

"Your money will be guaranteed by the government of South Africa. You will be acting on behalf of the SAI."

"That's more like it!" exclaimed Ian Hardy. "You were right, Ward. At least now we know which side is up."

"Damned right!" Ward agreed. "Now you got our attention. What's the story on this military compound?"

Carter turned to a crudely sketched map on the board behind him.

"The story is this. SWAPO has established a headquarters in Cassinga." He pointed to the area. "That would be here, just above Culevai. The compound itself is nothing special. It represents merely a point from which directives can be given and plans coordinated for what could be an invasion into Namibia."

"An invasion!" cried Shea. "So *that's* it!"

"And if you've come to the conclusion that it's Russian backed, you're probably right," he added. "Weapons have been pouring in off Soviet freighters for the past month. They land in Moçâmedes and are then shipped by rail to the interior of Angola. Our latest intelligence tells us that the weapons are already in place all along the border, so I'm going to give it to you straight: the invasion force is made up of about five thousand SWAPO troops and another two thousand Cubans. Air support will come from the Angolan army and perhaps even the Soviets. They will have Mirage jet fighters and Alouette choppers bought with Russian rubles from the French."

"So what's the good news?" joked Hardy. "We gotta have somethin' going for us, don't we?"

"What we have going for us is that we know the men leading this movement and their whereabouts. If we can get them out of the way, this will be just another collection of renegade guerrillas—well equipped guerrillas, I'll grant you, but factionalized and powerless once their leaders are neutralized."

"Who are their leaders?" Shea asked.

"The primary target is Colonel Theo Ithena, SWAPO's key man. If there is a successful invasion, the Soviets would most likely install him as president of Namibia. Without his presence, the Russians lose their legitimacy. Ithena has killed or imprisoned all of his rivals for the past decade with the exception of one man, Jonas Savimbi, who leads a group of rebels against the current regime of Eduardo dos Santos in Angola. Savimbi has been an outspoken critic of SWAPO but has been forced to live in the obscurity of the bush since 1976 when his party lost out to the Communists. Since that time, it has been Ithena and *only* Ithena. Without him SWAPO would be leaderless, with no recognized spokesman.''

Carter paused to gauge their reaction. Again there was none.

"The second man to be dealt with is a Soviet KGB officer. His name is Vladimir Andrei. A so-called 'advisor' working on behalf of the Angolan government, it was Andrei who first arranged sanctuary for the SWAPO guerrillas in Angola. He's sold his plan for a military takeover of Namibia to Angola's president—dos Santos—with the promise that he will share in the huge profits from the diamond mines there once Namibia is independent. The coordination of SWAPO's military forces are entirely dependent on Andrei. With him out of the way, we believe an effective attack will be impossible."

Carter scrutinized the faces of each of the six men. As before, their expressions were impossible to read. They gazed ahead, interested but uninspired. It was like talking to a window display of mannequins.

"Our third target is Carlos Ramirez," he continued, "the last in a long line of Cuban 'advisors' sent into Angola during the late 1970s. Ramirez is Castro's key man on the continent and is considered an expert on the psychology of the African mind. Appealing to their sense of patriotism and resentment at the early white exploitation of their countries, he has managed to foment discontent not only among Namibians, but among Angolans as well. Between them, Ramirez and

Andrei have managed to train a large and reasonably effective army. Even at this late date we can't be positive that Namibia is their target, but if it is, one thing is certain: the South-West African forces will be badly outnumbered."

The silence that followed was deafening as the small cadre of military men weighed the pros and cons of the undertaking. It was Van der Grif who finally spoke up.

"Your feelings concerning this mission—what are they?" he demanded. "Are you in or out?"

Shea turned around in his chair to face his five colleagues. As if through some unspoken code, he seemed to be soliciting the opinions of each. Finally he looked up from his seat to Van der Grif who stood looming over the table with wolfish anticipation.

"It ain't enough money."

Shea stood. He walked to the head of the table. Carter moved aside willingly as the big Rhodesian gave his version of what they'd be up against after having crossed the border into Angola. He was cocky, arrogant to a fault, Carter thought as he watched him. He drew a machete from his belt, then pointed with it to the border town of N'Giva.

"If there's going to be an invasion of Namibia, it will be launched from here," he began. "Air support can come from as far inland as Cassinga. There's an airstrip there capable of handling an operation like that, but as far as ground troops, tanks, copters, and the like, they'll be coming from N'Giva, Xangongo, and Mulemba. That's ten to twenty miles their side of the border.

"If these men are headquartered in Cassinga, we're going to have to pass through a wave of FAPLA, Cuban, and SWAPO troops. Worse, once we've completed our mission, we've got to pass through that same buildup again, but this time there'll be no element of surprise. Every revolutionary with a slingshot will be after our asses for at least a hundred miles. It's suicide! And I'm gonna tell you something; I ain't gonna buck those odds for no ten grand. It might be worth considering for twenty."

Carter watched Shea closely as he stood brazen and defiant, confident his cause would be furthered by the others. The man knew South Africa's position and knew the position of the United States as well. He and his men were desperately needed to avert what could prove to be a calamity for both nations. If Shea had even an inkling as to the real value of the Oranjemund mine, and its international implications, Carter was certain he'd be asking for five times the amount just requested. Still, they couldn't give in too easily. A quick "yes" would arouse Shea's suspicions.

"You've got it wrong, Shea," Carter said quietly. Carter took a step toward the map. "You've suggested the major towns along the border as points of entry, but any amateur would know that's exactly what we can't afford to do. The only border town we'll be near is Xangongo. If we can take the southern highway north, we can be within ten miles of Cassinga in one day. We can cover the remaining ten miles on foot by heading due east. I doubt there'll be any resistance. Furthermore, we won't go back the way we entered. *That* would be suicide." He drew a thick black line on the map. "From Cassinga we will head north five miles to Menongue. We can follow the railroad tracks to Moçâmedes where a ship will be waiting to give us passage home." He looked Shea dead in the eye. "Make sense?"

Shea swallowed hard. His cocky smile faded.

"Some," he answered. "But I still don't think it's enough money. You said yourself the country is loaded with Russians and Cubans. If those three creeps are as important as you say, they'll be guarded and guarded bloody damned well. This ain't gonna be easy, Carter. Besides, if we can stop a territory like Namibia from falling into the hands of the Russians, it's worth millions to South Africa."

Carter had played the role of devil's advocate. It was Van der Grif's part to concede to their demands.

"He has a point, Karl. What do you think?"

The major general was better at this than Carter had figured.

"Fifteen hundred per diem. A ten-thousand-dollar bonus if our adventure succeeds. That's the best I can do, and even that is beyond my authority."

The mercenaries seemed satisfied.

"I'm in," ventured Doc Barnes.

"Me too," echoed the New Zealanders.

"In," grumbled Ward.

"Sounds good to me," Chargas, the only Angolan among them, concluded.

Shea nodded slowly. He ran the palm of his hand over the side of his beard-stubbled face, then walked to the closed back room door. He swung it open.

"Boy!" he called in a Venda dialect. "Bring us some beer!"

He turned again to the group of them.

"If we're going to be fighting together, we might as well seal the deal with a round of drinks!"

Carter returned by plane to Pretoria late that night. The tentative date for their incursion into Angola was set for the following week. According to Van der Grif, it would take at least that long to organize the equipment necessary for the mission. This included many of the specialized weapons Shea and his men had insisted upon, plus provisions, and more importantly, a calculated plan of attack. Their intelligence, despite satellite photos provided by the Pentagon, was sketchy. Although they did know about the shiploads of weapons entering the country and even the positions of SWAPO training camps, security around the headquarters was still an unknown factor. Van der Grif was still hoping, it seemed, to hear something from his original fact-finding team sent to Cassinga nearly one week before. No word had come yet, and Carter was doubtful that any ever would. If they didn't get the information they were looking for, a diversion would be created in Botswana to draw attention away from their entry over the border. They would gladly take any advantage the South Africans could offer.

When Carter arrived at the Culembory Hotel, it was nearly two in the morning. His room there had become something of a permanent residence. Aubrey had been staying there since their recent brush with the KGB. He turned the key to the door, a feeling of comfortable familiarity welling within him at the thought of his new lover warm and inviting between the sheets. He pushed it open and was surprised to see Aubrey still awake, sipping from a glass of white wine.

She ran to him.

"Nick, you're back!"

Aubrey embraced him, and he kissed her.

"I didn't think you'd be coming back tonight. I was afraid something had happened."

"Nothing happened. We were just making some final arrangements," he whispered. "I've missed you."

They walked into the living room. Dressed in a thigh-length robe and without makeup, Aubrey appeared even more beautiful than he'd remembered.

"How is work going at the mine?"

She poured a glass of wine, and handed it to him.

"Most of the preliminary tests are being run here in Pretoria. Kallie Bloem had the kimberlite samples flown in this morning. It looks encouraging. It seems the Orange River once covered a far larger area than it does now. That makes it almost a certainty that the dry, subterranean river beds contain the diamonds we're after."

"And the alluvial mine?"

"It will be weeks before things get underway again there, I'm afraid, but we're hopeful."

He tasted the wine.

"Very nice. What is it?"

"Chenin Blanc. It comes from the Cape. Quite good, isn't it?"

Aubrey sat on the sofa across from him. He couldn't help but stare. He stepped toward her, then ran his fingers through her long, silky hair. It swept down below her shoulders now. She smiled, her eyes closed, content as a kitten.

"Is everything going well in Port Nolloth, Nick? Do you think this will all be over soon?"

He could only answer in generalities. Realizing one of the most crucial missions of his career lay just five days away, he felt obliged to lie.

"Yes. I think we've come up with a plan that will turn these recent setbacks around very quickly."

"And of course you can't tell me about it."

"No."

Aubrey reached for his hand. She kissed it.

"Good. I don't want to know because I'm certain that it's dangerous, and knowing could only worsen my fears. Sometimes I'm afraid for you, Nick. I don't know what you're going to do, but I have this horrible feeling. It's like a dream, except that it comes over me even when I'm awake. I'm afraid that you're going to die."

Carter leaned over to her and kissed her gently.

"Nothing bad is going to happen. If it did, I wouldn't be able to see you again, would I? And I could never let that happen. Not now."

They would go to bed that evening. They would make love as if it were for the last time. Tomorrow he would be in the offices of the SAI, plotting a triple assassination that promised to establish a winner in the U.S.–Soviet military stalemate for decades to come.

SEVEN

Theo Ithena was drunk as he wended his way into the barrack headquarters of the South-West African People's Organization. He carried a bottle of brandy in his right hand. In his left was an ivory walking stick with the revolutionary insignia carved into its handle. He stood laughing in sporadic giggles at the clever quips and anecdotes that passed silently through his mind. He believed in magic. Indeed, his father had been what the Europeans would call a witch doctor. To Ithena, his rise to success had been etched into the skies above by African gods more ancient than any man living or dead. He believed in destiny. Colonel Theo Ithena, head of the SWAPO organization of Namibia, was predestined to reign as emperor of a great African nation. This his father had foretold. And this was precisely what was coming to pass, he thought, lifting the bottle to his lips and pouring the strong liquor down his throat.

The men inside were of different civilizations: Russian, Cuban, and *mestiço*, a blend of Portuguese and Angolan. They could not understand the near religious purpose of his drunkenness. To Ithena, something more than success was at hand. The triumph of SWAPO's recent raids into South Africa represented more than just the physical act of terrorism. They represented the fulfillment of his father's prophesy and of his culture. The gods of Africa were alive! They were indeed watching over him and his country! He was as drunk from this knowledge as from the brandy.

Andrei, Ramirez and Kinshasa, the leader of the Angolan armed forces—FAPLA—did not share Ithena's convictions. They glowered from around the oval table where they were seated, silently watching the drunken man. And no one moved or said a word as the figurehead of African independence staggered forward, then launched into one of his all-too-frequent monologues. They stared at the tall, wiry African with the wild eyes as if he were some bizarre amusement.

Ithena rapped on the table with his long stick, swaying to and fro on this the most unlikely of theatrical stages.

"I had a vision today," he began. "In it there was an American. A white man. He has come to Africa to destroy me. He believes that Ithena is a bad man. Bad for Angola. Bad for Namibia. Bad for the United States."

The SWAPO leader leaned over the edge of the table. He bared his perfect teeth.

"This man must die," he vowed, "or Ithena and all of you will be killed in a river of bullets. This was my vision."

Andrei nodded. The antithesis of the colonel in appearance and philosophy, he was a medium-size, broad-shouldered man. He wore a thick black mustache. His normally waxen complexion was now crimson and peeling from his many months in the bush. A technician in every sense of the word, he'd have gladly put a bullet through the forehead of the man he gazed upon, but instead he smiled with the sincere look of an old and dear friend.

"I have told you before, Ithena. Every precaution has been taken. There is no danger. If this American were to come to Africa, he would regret the day he made such a decision. Our security is total, our plan of invasion impossible to stop."

Ithena raised his walking stick like a scepter.

"I have prayed for such a day. Ithena will not rest until the people of Namibia are liberated and the white devils of this continent turned to ashes. Already production at Oranjemund has been halted. The place of their sacrilegious technology—the electric station in Johannesburg—has been destroyed. I know this to be true. I saw it in a dream.''

The SWAPO leader paced the floor as if possessed by the very spirit of his visions. His eyes grew wide.

"Soon, control of the richest diamond reserves in all the world will be mine!"

The three men seated at the table were speechless. It was common for the colonel to assail them with such delusions of grandeur, but each time they were left afterward with only silence, a void that could just as easily be filled with laughter.

"Colonel Ithena," Ramirez said, "it is important that you sit with us to discuss plans for the invasion. Your soldiers will expect you to know. It is vital."

The revolutionary turned to him abruptly. He pulled a chair out from the table, then sat.

"Tell me now. I want to know."

The Cuban's gaze landed on the stack of handwritten notes that lay on the tabletop. He was unbathed and unshaven, but these were affectations as contrived as Ithena's. Beneath Ramirez's unkempt hair was a round, boyish face. He was no more than twenty-seven years old. He looked up from his notes.

"The attack will be a joint venture. It will begin with troop movements into Namibia spearheaded by artillery tanks and other armored vehicles. The drive will be supported by FAPLA aircraft. Jet fighters, Ithena, manned by Kinshasa's people. The tanks are the best, Russian made. Your soldiers have been well trained in their use. We will count on this first wave of artillery to cross the border from N'Giva through to Ondangua. From there it is a short run to Oranjemund, then on to Windhoek, the capital.''

"There is a territorial army in Namibia. How many do they number?"

It was Kinshasa who answered. Dressed in military khaki, his beret tilted to one side, he took the profession of soldiering more seriously than most.

"There are no more than two thousand South African

troops in Namibia now. The number was verified only this morning by Soviet intelligence.''

Ithena nodded. ''It is good. We will have little opposition. Besides, the Russians have promised air support once we reach Ondangua. Is that not true, Andrei?''

''Quite true,'' the Russian replied.

The SWAPO leader swiveled in his seat.

''Ramirez, your troops are ready?''

''Beyond a doubt.''

Ithena grinned broadly. His eyes were lit by a peculiar combination of madness and guile.

''The army of the South-West Africans has never been more eager to reclaim what is rightfully theirs. Ithena has rallied all the Marxists of Namibia, Botswana, and Angola into a unified fighting force.'' He slammed his walking stick onto the tabletop for emphasis. '' 'Woe on that day to the disbelievers! Begone to that hell which your heathen souls deny!' '' he quoted from the tribal writings of the Venda.

Once again, silence filled the room. For all of his eccentricity, mused Andrei, Theo Ithena knew his people. Braggart, drunkard, whoremonger, reciter of sacred scripture— he was all of these, but he understood what the blacks of his region wanted and he gave it to them. He had managed to maintain the fundamental truths of this most primitive society while projecting those truths into a modern Marxist philosophy.

''Ithena,'' Andrei whispered in a fervent voice, ''the invasion will take place one week from today.''

The SAI agent who stood watch over Aubrey Erhardt at the Culembory Hotel was sipping coffee from a ceramic mug when the two *mestiços* walked toward him. They were chatting in their native tongue, a dialect of Portuguese, as the South African eyed them suspiciously.

One of them drew a set of keys from his pocket, still talking in that rapid-fire dialect that sounded so alien to the agent. The men stood before a hotel room two doors down from the one where his charge resided. The South African pretended not to be watching as he touched the butt of the revolver that lay nestled beneath his armpit.

The man with the key raised his hand to the lock. The SAI agent sighed silently with relief—and the second *mestiço* reached for his weapon.

Two silenced rounds zipped into the guard's upper torso. The bullets passed through him, and four red holes sprouted from the flesh of his chest and back. He crumpled to the floor, and the two *mestiços*, acting quickly, frisked the dead man. A hotel key was in the pocket of his trousers. It was inserted into the lock. The door opened with a slight push as they entered the foyer, dragging the corpse behind.

Inside the hotel room, Aubrey Erhardt had just finished drawing water for a bath. She disrobed amid the warm steam of the tub and hypnotic rumble of running water. She thought she'd heard a sound from the other room but was uncertain. She wondered whether the SAI agent had returned for a refill of coffee.

"Wayne?" she called over the sound of the water. "Is that you?"

She listened for a moment. No response. She dismissed the sounds as products of her imagination, then stepped into the hot tub and twisted the faucets shut. Her attention returned to the bath. The luxury of the steaming tub was something she'd looked forward to since the early afternoon. Preliminary findings at the new Oranjemund site had been promising but were still a long way from conclusive. Both she and the corps of engineers she presided over had worked tirelessly in their attempt to locate the type 11-B diamonds, but no amount of effort could reverse overnight the damage done by SWAPO.

Aubrey lay back and closed her eyes. She ran a bar of perfumed soap from her outstretched foot to her calves, then up along her creamy thighs. The sensation made her think of Nick Carter. His name, his image seemed always to be with her, she realized. It took only a word or a phrase from a popular song to conjure up visions of him, until they whirled in her mind like a wondrous collage of their days and nights together. There was an excitement to her life that she hadn't experienced in years. Like an adolescent experiencing that first crush, there was a flavor of innocence and magic to it all.

Suddenly her reverie was shattered. Her eyes flashed open. There could be no mistake about it this time. She had heard a sound from outside the bathroom. Her body tensed. Her blue eyes widened with fear as the door opened. The two *mestiços* stood smiling in the doorway, guns drawn and pointed at her head.

"Very nice," the man closest to her commented, admiring her flawless physique.

Aubrey reached for a towel and covered herself instinctively.

"Who are you?" she demanded. "What do you want?"

"You will come with us, please," one of them answered.

She stood up angrily.

"I will not!" she protested. "You will leave this room immediately or I'll . . ." She hesitated.

"Or you will what?"

The man's eyes didn't blink. The stare smothered all resistance. She was incapable of speech.

"Put your clothes on. We will watch, and if you are lucky, that is all we will do. Do you understand? We are not here to hurt you. You are *muito inteligente*. The Russians want you for your knowledge of the blue stones from Oranjemund. It is not our wish to hurt you unnecessarily."

Aubrey swallowed hard and stepped from the bathtub. The towel dropped to the floor as she reached for her underwear. Her blue eyes were large and frightened; the eyes of the men were dark and voracious.

"Where are you taking me?" she asked, the words rushing from her mouth as she stepped into her panties.

The man who had done most of the talking thus far moved toward her, leaving his compatriot several steps behind. The second man snickered as he watched him grab her by the wrist.

"To heaven," he muttered before twisting her to one knee, then down onto the cold tile floor.

Two police cars and an ambulance were waiting with engines running and dome lights flashing as Carter entered the Culembory Hotel. A premonition of something having happened to Aubrey passed through Carter's mind like a dark shadow as he charged up the flights of stairs to his room. A flock of plainclothes detectives and SAI agents stood at the doorway, among them the ubiquitous Karl Van der Grif. He waved Carter off when he moved to enter, then clutched his arm and attempted to walk him in the opposite direction. Carter stopped abruptly.

"Is she dead?"

He looked hard into the major general's eyes.

"Is she dead?"

"No. But it serves no purpose to go in there. The technicians are going over the room for clues."

They began walking.

"Hurt, then? Answer me! What the hell is going on here, Karl?"

"Aubrey has been kidnapped, Nick. We have a good idea as to who did it and why."

Carter's chest heaved with a sigh of relief that Aubrey was alive.

"Where have they taken her?"

They walked down the stairs into the lobby. The cocktail lounge had closed hours ago, but they entered anyway.

Van der Grif walked behind the bar. He opened a bottle of scotch, then poured two glasses half full.

"Where have they taken her?" Carter repeated in an insistent whisper.

The major general lifted his glasses from his nose. He took them off and began wiping a lens with his handkerchief.

"Angola, perhaps. It would be insane for them to attempt taking her off the continent from any South African airport. They're all being watched. Wayne Albrecht's body was still

81

warm when we found him. Security was alerted immediately.''

Carter took a gulp of scotch. It warmed his hollow insides. For the moment, he felt like a gutted fish.

"You think she's headed for Moscow?"

"Where else? The Soviets wanted her badly. Aubrey is a valuable commodity to them, Nick. More valuable than you can imagine." The muscles in his face tensed as he stared into Carter's eyes. "You are aware of Dirk Erhardt's position among the scientific elite of his time?"

"I know about the work he'd done with laser weaponry, if that's what you mean."

"It is, but there's more to it than that. You see, Aubrey was present as an adolescent during much of her father's research into military uses for the boron-coated diamonds. Of course, no significant reserve of the gems existed at that time, but he recognized that someday—long after the vacuum tubes of the 1950s and the silicate chips and transistors of the 1970s and 1980s—high-resistivity diamonds would be made or discovered. Well, they have.''

"Which makes the research he did a decade ago pretty important.''

"Precisely."

"Did Aubrey have access to it?"

Van der Grif sighed audibly. The life seemed to drain from his body. He appeared, in fact, to be immersed in failure.

"She may, though I cannot say for certain. Her father was doing his work under the aegis of the South African government, but no one could appreciate his genius then. No one with the exception of the Germans with whom he'd collaborated years earlier. There were several rather generous offers, but he rejected them all. After an abortive kidnap attempt not unlike Aubrey's, he destroyed his notes on how to make the diamonds operational. It was shortly thereafter that he was killed in a terrorist bombing.''

"His research is lost?"

"That is what we assumed, but now our intelligence

people have come up with another theory."

He looked down to the mahogany bar. He was somber and embarrassed.

"We now think he passed this information along to his daughter before he died."

"Aubrey? She'd have told you!"

"Only if she knew, Nick, but we don't think she did. Since her kidnapping tonight, our people believe the core of Dirk Erhardt's work was conveyed to her as a teen-ager while in an hypnotic trance. It would still be there, clear as on a printed page, etched on the subconscious of that young woman."

Carter studied the security officer; the man's face was ashen with nerves and fatigue. The theory, as unbelievable as it sounded, made sense. Who would suspect that the most vital military secret since the splitting of the atom had been indelibly inscribed on the mind of a teen-age girl? In retrospect, it didn't take much figuring to know why Van der Grif wanted this conversation private. The revelation both amazed and angered Carter.

"Then why the hell wasn't she better protected?"

"Because we didn't know!" Van der Grif retorted. "We tried to convince her that this wasn't the best place for her, but she wouldn't listen to us. She wasn't our prisoner, so we assigned her a guard. The next step would have been a military compound, but we had no idea then as to what she might know. Besides, we needed her at Oranjemund."

Carter's silence told Van der Grif more than any words could. The Killmaster felt as if he were personally to blame for Aubrey's kidnapping.

The major general finished his scotch in a prolonged swallow, then placed the glass on the bar. He poured them both another.

"If it's any consolation, we're almost certain she's still alive. Aubrey is too valuable to let die."

Carter sipped slowly from his glass. The scotch burned as he sloshed it around inside his mouth, savoring the heat, the burning heat of the scotch and his anger.

"You're in love with her, aren't you?" Van der Grif asked at last.

Carter looked up from his glass.

"I didn't want to see her get involved, Karl! We're sitting on a powder keg, you know that. The survival of this society is hanging by a thread. SWAPO is just the beginning, and that's what should scare you. If they're successful in Namibia, it will set off a chain reaction that will end in a bloodbath for all of South Africa. That thread is already frayed. The blacks of this continent have realized their destiny and will stop at nothing to see it fulfilled. They don't care about diamonds or satellite warfare, and as long as Aubrey is among them, her life could not be in more danger!"

Van der Grif's glasses reflected the dim morning light so that Carter could no longer see his eyes. Still, Carter knew that his expression was intense and sincere as he responded.

"Then for both her sake and yours, I pray she is en route to Russia. At least she will be safe there."

A heavy silence followed as they found themselves pondering the significance of the events that had unfolded over the past couple of days. Aubrey Erhardt had been kidnapped. There was now hard evidence to suggest that SWAPO, under the direction of Vladimir Andrei, was about to launch an invasion of Namibia. Just when, they could not determine, but the cornerstone of their strategy rested in a covert operation that would remain hidden from the rest of the world: the planners of the Namibian invasion would be neutralized, their puppet leader liquidated. All of this to keep a handful of rare, boron-coated diamonds accessible to the United States and out of the Soviet Union's grasp.

"I haven't seen a paper in two days. How are things going in New York?"

Van der Grif shrugged.

"One of our newspapers would do you little good on that score. Few people here are aware of the United Nations vote. The news is censored, but word is that there will be a vote next week. SWAPO has made its case. A convincing one. The U.S. has promised to abstain.''

"What about South Africa? Are the members of the General Assembly aware of the military buildup beyond your borders?''

"Charges and countercharges. They claim that we are escalating.'' He shook his head disgustedly. "At times I feel it's hopeless. A diplomatic chess game we stand no chance of winning.''

Carter analyzed the situation as it existed. Given the handful of men involved in their mission, it was pointless to wait any longer. The odds against their success were mounting with the passage of time. Whether the operation was successful or not would have little bearing on the vote for an economic boycott of South Africa.

"Karl, I'd like to step up the timetable for our move into Angola. I think we should proceed within the next forty-eight hours. Is that possible?''

"Are you certain Aubrey's situation isn't forcing your hand?'' Van der Grif asked.

"Don't be ridiculous! What it adds up to is this: the longer we wait, the more time Andrei has to set up. We don't know when SWAPO is planning its strike into Namibia, but once it begins, our chance of containing it is over. We must get to the principals involved before that, or we're finished. South Africa is engaged in a confrontation with SWAPO, FAPLA, and the Soviets. It's a conflict your country can't hope to win.''

The head of South African security yielded to Carter's logic.

"The weapons have already been obtained. The plan—for all its danger—is valid, and the men are seasoned professionals. I don't see why it can't be pushed forward if that is what you want.''

"It is.''

"Consider it done,'' concluded Van der Grif, polishing off the last of his scotch.

He pushed the bottle forward.

"This is for you. My working day began yesterday morning at six. It appears it's begun again just now after only a two-drink hiatus."

"When will I hear from you?"

"Tonight. I shall arrange schedules with Shea and the others. If they are in agreement, supplies will be waiting in Ondangua by tomorrow morning."

"I appreciate that, Karl. You don't know how much."

The men shook hands, and Van der Grif left the Culembory bar to Carter and his solitary ruminations.

Carter poured himself two fingers of scotch. His thoughts lingered on Aubrey. He could have prevented her being kidnapped simply by *being* there. But he wasn't. Nor had he taken the precaution of booking her a separate room in another hotel far from Pretoria. It was his fault, and the notion tormented him. True, she was probably still alive. The Soviets needed her expertise in order to exploit the Oranjemund find. He was convinced that she had been taken from South Africa and was now in Angola, perhaps even in Cassinga where the SWAPO forces made camp.

Carter took a swig from his glass. It would take only a shower and shave to put him back on track again, but for the moment he wanted only to think. He wanted to remember Aubrey and the conversations and the lovemaking they'd shared. He wanted to put this mission in perspective again, to examine it carefully, because if he died, he wanted to feel sure that there was more to his decision than private motives. Aubrey was a prize for whatever country procured the knowledge she possessed. Her father had achieved results working on the most advanced weapons known to modern man. With the discovery of the type 11-B diamonds in Oranjemund, those theories became the most devastating reality imaginable. If Aubrey Erhardt's safety was important to him personally, she was now far more vital to the security of his country.

Carter downed the remainder of his drink. His bet was that

if they moved now, they could catch Andrei in advance of the invasion. If that happened, they stood a reasonable chance of freeing Aubrey before she left the continent. Anything less than that on either score would represent the most dismal kind of failure to him both as a man and an AXE agent.

EIGHT

Nick Carter heard from Van der Grif later that morning. Shea and his men would be arriving at Ondangua in a matter of hours. The weapons and supplies were already in place. That was all he needed. The major general had arranged for air transport to the tiny border town via an Impala chopper. They met at a small private airfield just outside of Pretoria that same day.

When Carter exited his cab, Van der Grif was waiting for him. His gear had been provided by the SAI, all of it foreign: French boots, East German canteens, Russian weapons and khaki. The remainder was already packed. The helicopter pilot was warming the engines about two hundred feet from them as Van der Grif bade him farewell.

"This is it, Nick. I realize we haven't known one another very long, but I want you to know that I admire you and what you're doing. You are a great patriot."

Carter smiled thinly. The wind stirred by the rotors formed a cloud of dust that hung above the barren strip thirty miles outside the capital. Even in a setting as improbable as this, Van der Grif looked the part of a gentleman. With his hair blowing in every direction and his bespectacled countenance covered with brownish-yellow dust, he still maintained a dignity Carter had come to know and respect.

"I appreciate that, Karl. Coming from you, it means a lot."

They shook hands warmly. Then Van der Grif pulled Carter forward and patted his back.

"You know the arrangement. You are embarking now on a phase of this mission where neither my government nor yours can be of any assistance. You are on your own. A man with no country."

He handed Carter a billfold. It contained a passport, driver's license, proof of inoculation, and four hundred dollars worth of Angolan currency.

"Your identity from here on will be that of Robert Sublett. You are a freelance writer doing a book on the success of the dos Santos revolution in Angola. Your papers will reflect that. The others involved have been supplied similar identification in the event they are killed or captured."

Carter pulled away from him.

"We'll meet again," he called over the roaring Impala engines. "We'll drink to the success of this mission!"

The copter pilot waved Carter on as he bent low under the churning rotor. He boarded, and they were in the air and headed for Ondangua in a matter of seconds. Below them he could see Van der Grif. The major general stood watching to the last instant of visibility, a solitary figure against the barren African plain.

The rendezvous point for the seven-man team was just north of Ondangua. A bivouac of two small tents had been constructed. Carter hoped the mercenaries had spent the night reviewing the details of the plan and familiarizing themselves with the equipment. Shea, Ward, and Barnes greeted him as the copter came to rest a short distance from the camp.

Carter grabbed his gear, and jumped from the doorway. Even as he trotted from the craft, the pilot was taking her up again, eager to leave a zone rife with military clashes between terrorists and the South African Territorial Force. Carter glanced over his shoulder as the copter drifted away at a forty-five-degree angle, realizing that that was the last contact he would have with any organized military ally.

"Carter!" Shea roared as he approached the tents. "I was glad to hear you're so anxious to begin. It's been nearly three months since our last assignment. My men are ready."

Shea followed Carter into one of the tents.

"Supplies all here?" Carter asked, tossing his knapsack on the ground.

Shea spread his arms and grinned.

"Everything we asked for. The tent was full of weapons ranging from 120mm mortars and ILUM bazookas to Soviet-made AK-47 rifles and grenades."

Carter's eyes fell upon Barnes who stood hovering over a crate containing plastic explosives.

"How're you doin', Doc?"

"Never better!" The black man replied, beaming. "I got what I want. Everything. There ain't nothin' we can't do now, and you can believe that with ol' Doc around!"

"Good. What about you, Ward? You satisfied with the equipment they've provided?"

Anthony "One Shot" Ward lifted a .45-caliber, 9mm submachine gun. He held it at waist level like most people would hold a kitten. Comfortable with its feel, he nodded his satisfaction.

"It's all here, Carter, just like you said. I got no kicks with nobody."

Enrico Chargas, Peter Wesson, and Ian Hardy entered, their faces covered with burnt cork.

"And you men? Everything okay?"

"*Sim,*" said Chargas. He drew his passport from his pants pocket. "Beginning today, I am Ernesto Garcia, a Portuguese salesman." He looked up from the papers with a quick grin. "How 'bout you?"

"Robert Sublett, a freelance writer," Carter answered. "And you?" he asked Peter Wesson.

The New Zealander glanced at his identification.

"Brian Smithers, a university professor."

Hardy followed suit. "David Abercrombie, Esquire, a British barrister."

Doc Barnes seemed to be enjoying the exercise. "Jo-Jo White, a professional basketball player," he announced.

"Larry Engels, a travel agent from the States," Ward continued.

A silence ensued. All heads turned to Shea who sat silently chewing a wad of tobacco.

"Hey, Shea! What's your ID say?" Barnes asked good-naturedly.

The mercenary leader spat a yellow stream onto the ground.

"I don't like games. Not when I'm gettin' ready for a job."

He stood, then made his way toward the tent flaps.

"James Elliot," he stated without inflection, "American in the oil business."

The men looked at one another as he left. His presence seemed to have left a vibration in the air.

"Let's get the hell out of here," Carter suggested. "What kind of ground transportation do we have?"

"A Land-Rover and a military jeep," answered Hardy, following him as he walked from the tent.

"Fine. Load 'em up. We'll need provisions for at least a week. I want the metal detector kept in the lead vehicle. I hear the southern highway is loaded with land mines."

"Right-o," the New Zealander said.

Carter stood in the middle of the camp, watching the six men begin to load the two vehicles. There was an unspoken tension even among these veterans of battle. It was evidenced in the uneasy laughs and conscious swaggering. Shea, with his gruff bark of a voice, needled the easy-going New Zealanders. Doc Barnes, placid as a mountaintop, was an ocean of pent-up anger waiting to vent itself in one volcanic blast of flame and destruction. Ward clung to his submachine gun like a little girl to a favorite rag doll. Peter Wesson, his arms full of tattoos, worked with his sidekick, Ian Hardy, who was always eager to please, his face now blackened, his blue eyes sparkling with excitement as he loaded crates into the Land-Rover.

It was a motley crew, Carter thought, but a competent and determined one as well. All things being equal, he'd always had a preference for working in small numbers. It was more efficient, less complicated. Watching them now, he had the feeling they might actually have a chance at beating the odds, of striking at the Achilles heel of this Soviet adventure and living to tell about it.

Shea stood before him once the supplies had been loaded.

"We're set to go," he growled. "Ain't no time like the present, is there, sir?"

Carter scrutinized the middle-aged mercenary. At first skeptical of Carter's credentials, Shea had no doubt reconsidered. Carter didn't correct him on the "sir." Shea was a pro; once the contract had been signed, it was strictly military, especially when it came to the chain of command.

"Then what are we waiting for? Let's get our asses over the border before daylight."

"Yes, sir!" he responded, turning to the others. "All right, guys. You've got your assignments. Let's move out!"

The seven of them manned the two vehicles. Shea, Chargas, and Carter led in the jeep. Barnes, Ward, and the two New Zealanders followed in the Land-Rover, which held most of the equipment. Their goal was clear from the beginning. Since they knew that troops were already in N'Giva, they would slip over the border just west of there, then continue along the southern highway to Xangongo and finally to Cassinga, where South African intelligence had placed SWAPO headquarters.

By moonlight, the group moved without incident along a narrow dirt road that cut through the bush. Even the unpaved South African roads seemed good when compared to the uncleared back roads that lay ahead. They averaged about thirty-five miles an hour until they arrived at the border.

Civil war had been raging in Angola for nearly fifteen years, and though the Marxist regime of Eduardo dos Santos claimed control of the government, South African-backed rebels under the command of Jonas Savimbi thrived in the southernmost regions of Namibia. Evidence of this was the wooden signpost that marked the border crossing. It had been defaced with the words *Morte a dos Santos* scribbled in black paint over the barely discernible words announcing entry into the Republic of Angola. The jeep led the way over the border without headlights.

"We must be careful now," urged Chargas. "Since this is where the rebels hide, the roads are full of mines."

Carter brought the jeep to a halt. Chargas stepped out, taking the metal detector with him. He flicked it on.

"Follow me, but slowly. Stick to the exact path that I am walking, and tell the others to do the same."

Shea and Carter watched as the Angolan led the way on foot. It was a painstaking process, but one that would be necessary for the next couple of miles. No one understood that better than Enrico Chargas. He was what was known as a *pica*. The word, derived from the lance used by bullfighters, seemed appropriate as he probed the ground ahead with the hand-held electronic device. They passed a three-quarter-ton truck whose passengers had not been so cautious. Turned over on its side, with its front axle and cab blown to pieces, it was a grim reminder to others that all was not well in the Republic of Angola.

They had gone only about three hundred yards when Chargas stopped suddenly. The red light on the metal detector flashed wildly as he passed the device in front of him, then to his left and right. He swung around to the others.

"This is it," he whispered. "A string of them."

"What now?" asked Shea.

"We must dig them out, then detonate them electronically."

"Oh, that's great," the big mercenary muttered.

"Barnes!" he bellowed. "Get up here!"

The tall American loped to the side of the jeep.

"Yes, sir?"

"Chargas thinks he's found a string of land mines up ahead. Can you detonate them?"

Barnes grinned broadly. "Ain't no problem, sir."

Doc Barnes walked up to Chargas, who was picking through the layer of gravel that covered the road. The Angolan moved from one mine to the other, carefully clearing the loose gravel away with a thin wooden plank.

Barnes lay flat on his belly beside him. He dared not use a flashlight in case the mines were magnetic. He examined one in the pale moonlight. As he'd suspected, it was of Soviet manufacture. He got to his feet as Chargas was brushing away the dirt that buried the last of them.

Barnes walked back to the jeep.

"What's the story?" Carter asked.

"Story is, they're Russian mines. TM-46s like the Tellermines the Germans used in World War Two."

"Can you detonate them?"

"Sure I can. The problem is there'll be one hell of an explosion."

"Is it possible to defuse them?"

"It's possible, but it's mighty dangerous. They're magnetic, so any tool I use would set 'em off. If you ask me, it'd be best to just let 'em blow."

Carter turned to Shea.

"What do you think?"

"Doesn't sound like we got much choice, does it, sir?"

Carter shot a glance into the sky. The moon, like a big pale eye, hid itself behind some scudding clouds, then reappeared once more. The last thing they needed was to announce their arrival to the FAPLA.

"Get Chargas over here," he ordered.

The Angolan was there in an instant.

"Sir?"

"What are the odds of us going around this string of mines, off the road, and through the bush for a couple of hundred feet?"

"I don't think so. These mines were set up by FAPLA counterinsurgence forces. I am not the first man to think of using a metal detector. The area that borders this trap is surely mined as well."

"Then it's decided," Carter stated soberly. "Barnes! Do what you have to do. Hardy! Back up that Land-Rover. Let's get the hell out of the way!"

He and Hardy reversed their paths, careful to retrace the same cleared pattern they'd followed while moving forward. Barnes stood fifty yards ahead. All watched as he raised a .30-caliber carbine, then shouted, "When this mother blows, they'll all blow!" With that, he took aim at the first in a string of seven TM-46 land mines. He fired, and the first mine detonated, beginning a chain of explosions that shook the ground around them and rocketed fiery balls of molten shrapnel into the sky above.

The seven men stood silent and still, awaiting any signal that enemy troops might respond. An eerie quiet followed. Carter scanned the winding dirt road and the bush that surrounded it. Chargas was standing beside him. The Angolan's gun was raised. His right eye was twitching.

"How much more of this can we expect, Chargas?"

"Only the FAPLA convoys know where the mines have been buried. There may or may not be more, so we must continue in the same way we started. The mines were planted here to protect the bridge at the Cunene River."

"How much further is that?"

"Another mile at least."

Carter grimaced. "That will be all for now, Chargas," he said, dismissing him. "Carry on with the search. You're doing a good job."

The Angolan trotted up ahead, passed Barnes, and walked slowly into the mined zone that stretched before them. Carter's eyes fixed on Shea.

"I want you and Hardy to follow behind the jeep on foot. I want Barnes and Ward to trail the Land-Rover. Watch the roadside in case of an ambush. When you leave a calling card like the one we just did, you're bound to get some company."

"You've got it," agreed Shea, hopping from the jeep.

With two-man teams trailing each vehicle and Enrico Chargas leading the way, their entry into Angola continued at a snail's pace.

If there was a specific locale where they were almost certain to encounter resistance, it was near the crude wooden bridge that joined the banks of the Cunene River. Strategic in the sense that most of the troops headed for the border would be crossing it, FAPLA would be vigilant in its effort to protect it. Carter and the other men counted on this, and they deviated from the main highway about a quarter mile south. Considering the land mines, it was a dangerous move, but their options were limited. They would either take that risk or find themselves in the middle of an ambush from which there could be no possible escape.

The drudgery of the trek toward Cassinga was torturous. Enrico Chargas, whose guts and skill they depended upon, was feeling the strain. Perspiration poured from his forehead and temples. His round, sunburned face was a mask of concentration as he led the mercenary platoon forward. Step by slow step, they watched from behind as Chargas led them north toward the river. The silence was unnerving. For the third time since they'd crossed the border, they came upon the bloody and scattered remains of an impala that had detonated one of the TM-46s. Other impala observed quietly as vultures swooped down and ripped bits of flesh from sections of bone that were strewn around them. Like those surviving members of the herd, the mercenaries looked at one another, realizing that death lay just one step away in the wrong direction. At last, Chargas turned to them.

"This is it!" he exhorted in an excited whisper. "The river lies just beyond this clearing!"

None of them in the lead jeep had time to respond as a single, crackling explosion sounded, and the Angolan's body was thrown like a rag doll into the air, then dropped to the ground some fifteen feet from them.

"Chargas!" Carter cried, but even this involuntary shout was interrupted by a barrage of enemy fire.

Their crawl forward came to an abrupt halt. For a moment, they were all stunned, but then Carter jumped from the jeep, firing a salvo of bullets from the machine gun he brandished. Wesson leaped from the Land-Rover, discharging a clip of .45-caliber slugs with equal vehemence. In a split second, each of them was in fighting position. The soldiers of FAPLA, who were known to be notoriously bad shots, lived up to their reputation. No one had been hit. Together they crouched behind the Land-Rover and jeep.

Shea's eyes were sharp and racing as he stared ahead into the thick underbrush that bordered the clearing they had entered.

"The fire is coming from the bush. They must have been laying for us."

"Well, at least we're not locked in a crossfire. Ward!" Carter bellowed.

Ward duck walked to Carter. A volley of machine gun fire followed him. Some passed overhead, but the majority ripped into the jeep and Rover. Carter saw three of the four exposed tires go flat, then he answered with his own vicious assault.

"Sir?"

"Fire is coming from just one direction. Can you make out from where?"

"Yeah. I can see just fine."

"If we pin them down to that area, can you send in a mortar? It'll have to be soon. We have no time to calibrate the launcher. It's gotta be one shot, or they'll scatter."

The mercenary's overdeveloped upper trunk heaved. His eyes shone as the edges of his handlebar mustache tugged upward.

"They do call me One Shot, now, don't they, sir?"

Carter turned to the others as Ward moved to ready his mortar.

"Fire away!" he ordered. "Shoot wide to either side. We want to keep them right where they are!"

On that command, the group let loose with everything that they had. The attack was sustained, but not unanswered. Their bullets were returned one for one and with equal determination. But this game was theirs. They had only to keep the FAPLA troops preoccupied and in one place for a few seconds longer.

Once Ward had scrambled back to the Land-Rover, he lifted his right arm, then reached above him for the 120mm mortar. He pulled it down, then spiked its square pad into the dirt. He loaded it, and his clear, discerning eye gauged the distance from where the fire emanated. He determined the arc and range, then glanced across a latice of gun barrels to Carter. He nodded. The first rocket shot high into the air, falling amid the thorn and baobab trees with the grace of a discus. They knew immediately that the shot was good, because along with the earth and greenery, pieces of equipment and parts of bodies were hurled in all directions. The briefest of respites followed before they peppered the entire area with machine gun fire. Doc Barnes ran forward for the cleanup, pitching two grenades into the thicket. Chest heaving, his advance stopped at the lip of the clearing. His dark eyes were intense as he motioned them forward.

"They're all dead now," he muttered, peering into the mass of shrubs and trees and vines. "All of them."

The others joined Barnes as Carter ran to Enrico Chargas. The brave *pica* was still breathing, but just barely. His left foot had been blown off. His entire upper torso was punctured with deep shrapnel wounds. Carter knelt beside him, examining what were certainly mortal wounds. In his delirium, Chargas was talking to his mother in Portuguese.

"It's all right, Chargas," Carter comforted. "It will all be over soon."

Shea walked toward his stricken comrade. He drew a Luger from his gun belt.

"Is he going to make it?"

Carter shook his head. Shea cocked his weapon.

"I know him, Carter. He'd want it this way."

Carter took a final look at Chargas as he writhed in the dirt, mumbling through bloody lips. He stood.

"Do it."

A solitary shot rang out. The sound of it made the others turn in their direction. They stood silent for a moment, jarred from the frenzy they'd experienced while raking through the cache of FAPLA supplies.

"Don't get too worked up over all of that," Carter instructed. "We'll be on foot from here on. You keep it, you carry it."

Reluctantly, the three mercenaries dropped the Russian-made weapons they'd uncovered as Ward made the rounds, picking the Angolan corpses clean of rings, cash, and other valuables. Afterward, they unloaded what they could from the jeep and Land-Rover, then plodded west toward the Cunene River.

Despite the short distance to the river, their pace was cautious. There was none among them who took what had happened to Chargas lightly, and it was dusk by the time they reached its bank. Each was flat on his belly when the bridge came into sight. Ian Hardy was the first to speak.

"Will you look at that?" he gasped. "There must be a thousand troops!"

It was, more or less, the same thought that passed through all their minds as they watched, mesmerized, by the procession of Communist forces that marched along the rickety structure.

"Christ, Carter, the invasion has already begun!"

NINE

Aubrey Erhardt's gait was unsteady as the Cuban guard led her from her quarters to the austere, split-level building that served as SWAPO headquarters. Her feet were bare, her dress soiled and torn at the shoulder.

The soldier clutched one arm, pulling her along.

"Move it!" he ordered rudely.

The geologist was too exhausted to react. Her eyes floated to the back of her head. Her footsteps were dragging now. Her thinking was languid and confused. She understood that she was in the Cassinga compound that housed the leaders of SWAPO, but why? What was it they wanted from her?

They stepped onto a platform constructed of unpainted wooden planks. The cadence of the soldier's heavy boots sounded loud and sharp as they walked toward the headquarters office. The Cuban opened the door with one hand as he shoved her forward with the other.

Aubrey was startled to see the amount of radio equipment, radar, and maps that filled the room. Two men were seated across from one another at a rectangular conference table. One was medium-size and rather handsome with a thick black mustache. He was clad in military fatigues. The second looked to be in his late fifties. Intellectual in appearance, he was smaller and wore horn-rimmed glasses. She recognized neither.

101

"You wanted to see the girl," the Cuban stated.

"Yes," the younger of the two men responded. "The lady will kindly have a seat. Felipe, you will stay here in case you are needed."

The soldier cast his charge a lethal glance as she stepped forward. It was a hard, taunting gaze, the kind she had become accustomed to during her short stay in Angola. She was persona non grata, a South African.

Aubrey approached the two men and took a seat at the end of the table. Her eyes were wary as she attempted to assess her captors. From their appearance and accent, she gathered both were Russian.

"My name is Vladimir Andrei," said the man with the mustache, extending his hand.

She clasped it limply.

"And this is Boris Troyansky. Comrade Troyansky is a scientist like you, Miss Erhardt. Like you."

The gemologist nodded a greeting. Andrei's expression grew speculative.

"You have been treated well these past three days?"

Aubrey's mind shot back over the seventy-two hours of hell she had experienced: the men who had brutalized her in Pretoria; the lack of food and sleep; fetid quarters. Her chin quivered.

"Well," he rationalized, "these are men at war. Surely you cannot expect the comforts of Johannesburg here in the bush."

Andrei reached for a dossier that rested on the tabletop.

"In any case, you are here and appear to me to be in good health. That is what is important, for soon you will be leaving these, shall we say, rugged environs for the comforts of one of the world's most beautiful cities." He flashed a smile in her direction. "Before you leave, however, it is necessary for me to ask you certain questions that my superiors feel must be answered immediately. Shall we begin?"

He glanced across the metal table to the Soviet gemologist. Boris Troyansky moved his chair closer to her. He smiled a short, impish grin.

THE BLUE ICE AFFAIR

"Miss Erhardt, we have analyzed samples of the diamonds recently uncovered at Oranjemund and are very interested in them. While worthless as gemstones because of the blue impurities that run through them, they are of interest to my government for other reasons." He hesitated. "As I suspect you know, the trace quantities of the element boron present in them have altered their electrical properties making them semiconductors with a resistivity on the order of a hundred OHMS. They also have light-transmission qualities that make them valuable in the field of computers and microelectronics. Are these terms familiar to you?"

The right side of Aubrey's face was badly swollen. When she answered, her words came out a muted whisper.

"They are, but it isn't computer technology that makes the stones important. Your government wants them to make weaponry, laser beam weaponry that can be fired at the speed of light from unmanned satellites that the Soviet Union has had in position for years."

The gemologist nodded slowly.

"That is all quite true. Laser weapons will make the American ICBM and MX missiles obsolete. Traveling at a speed of seventeen thousand miles per hour, they will appear dinosaurs when compared to the hundred eighty-six thousand miles per second of a laser. That is why we are talking, then, is it not?"

"You would know more about those subjects than I, Mr. Troyansky. I am a geologist. It isn't difficult to identify the gems. You already have. You know their source and their application. What else is there to know?"

Troyansky's thin face tightened. The skin of his face contracted so that he appeared another man, a man obsessed with the need for information as other men might be obsessed with money or drugs.

"In order to be of practical value, the boron-coated diamond must be enhanced in much the same manner as uranium. Without this enhancement, the stones are nitrogen poor and of no use to us. It was your father who perfected that method—in theory, at least. His years of research have now

103

become most important to the Soviet government. We would pay you handsomely for any light you could shed on those findings.''

Aubrey stared at the man. "I was twelve years old when my father was involved with those experiments! Do you think he told me? Do you honestly think I'd remember even if he did?" She gave a short, harsh laugh.

Andrei leaned forward on the table.

"So you have no recollection concerning his work?"

"Don't be ridiculous," she snapped. "I was a little girl at the time! Is this why you've brought me here? If it is, you are all quite insane. I have no knowledge whatsoever concerning my father's theories on enhancement!"

Andrei scrutinized her. He stared deep into her frightened eyes, evaluating her words and reactions.

"Shall we torture you?"

Her head lowered. The hours of isolation and lack of sleep had taken their toll.

"I tell you I don't know!" she cried out at last. "What good will torturing me do you if I don't know? Why can't you believe that?"

"I do believe you," he said in a soft voice, "but we must be certain."

A moment of silence followed. The appraising stares of both men focused on her.

"What are you going to do with me?" she asked in a small voice.

Andrei walked across the room. He opened a small refrigerator, producing a filled syringe.

"Nothing painful," he said, depressing the plunger so that a bit of the clear liquid spurted from the tip of the hypodermic. "A simple test. Mental, not physical. No pain. No lengthy interrogations. Just a method of discerning truths that you yourself may be unaware you carry hidden within your subconscious. If you do not have the information we need, you will be imprisoned temporarily, then released. If you do, you are a most valuable asset to the Communist world, Miss

Erhardt, and will be transported to Moscow without delay."

He strode across the room, then stood before her. He reached for her arm. She flinched.

"What is it?"

"Sodium aminate. Quite harmless. A favorite tool of the KGB and your SAI as well. It will free your mind and your tongue so that you can discuss these childhood memories without prodding. Wonderful, isn't it? Science, I mean. It can make even the most unpleasant of duties . . . clean. You go uninjured, and we derive the information we require at the same time."

He bent over her.

"Extend your arm, please."

"I will not."

"Felipe," he called.

The Cuban guard stepped forward.

"Hold her arm steady."

The soldier wrenched her arm back and pulled up her sleeve until the roundness of her shoulder was exposed. Andrei administered a 50cc dose of the drug, then withdrew the needle.

"And now we wait," he said, waving his subordinate away from her.

The three men present observed Aubrey for a period of ninety seconds. She felt nauseated and dizzy. A veil of perspiration covered her burning face.

"How are you feeling?" asked the KGB man.

His words echoed in her mind as if through a cavern of memories and experiences. Andrei's face and the faces of Troyansky and Felipe seemed suddenly unreal, altering in size and appearance from one moment to the next.

"I feel sleepy and awake at the same time."

"The drug is taking effect," Troyansky observed. "We should begin, no?"

"Go on," Andrei agreed.

The gemologist hovered over Aubrey, his face just inches from her as he spoke.

"Miss Erhardt," the scientist began, "when you were young and your father was alive, you took an interest in his work. We know this," he added, "to be a fact. We know also that he passed along certain information about the work he was doing; he had you commit certain vital facts to memory."

The KGB man seemed impatient with Troyansky's prattling.

"These facts had to do with boron-coated diamonds, Miss Erhardt," Andrei interrupted. "Do you remember discussing these diamonds with your father?"

"Yes," she answered numbly.

"What did you discuss, Miss Erhardt? What information did he give you?"

"He told me that the blue diamonds had special properties. He told me that they were used because they could withstand extremely high temperatures and electrical intensity. He called them conductors, 'superconductors,' I think."

"Correct! That is quite correct, Miss Erhardt! What else did he tell you? What did he tell you about enhancing the blue diamonds so that they become superconductors?"

The young woman fell silent. The inner workings of her mind seemed all but transparent as she strained under the influence of the sodium aminate.

"I do not know," she finally admitted.

"But you have to know!" Troyansky urged. "We know that he told you! He had no alternative but to tell you once his notes were destroyed!"

Andrei winced at the gemologist's outburst. He motioned him away.

"Miss Erhardt, I want you to try very hard to remember. We believe that you do have this information but were instructed not to tell us. Of course, that is absurd. We are your friends, Aubrey, and you must tell us all that you know."

Aubrey's face became illuminated with the radiance of revelation.

"You may be right in what you say. Perhaps my father did

106

tell me something, but I cannot say what it was. I can feel it there—the information, I mean—as if it were in a vault somewhere deep in my mind, but the vault is locked and I cannot get to it. I cannot *touch* it. It's like it may be there, but it is a shadow with no substance to touch.''

"Try, Miss Erhardt," Troyansky implored. *"You've got to try!"*

"I am, I tell you!" she screamed back at him. *"I am!!"*

"Enhancement! Think of that word! Remember, Aubrey, remember when you were a little girl and your father was alive. Can you remember that?"

"Yes, I remember," she responded, sounding suddenly fatigued.

"Your father must have been very busy at that time. He was on the verge of a great scientific breakthrough on which he had worked many months. Is that true?"

Aubrey's head lowered.

"Yes."

"You have already told us about the blue diamonds and how they are used as semiconductors. You also told us that these gems could be enhanced, that is, made into superconductors capable of laser beam light transmission."

Andrei monitored her reactions to his prodding. He inspected the subtleties of her expression: her eyes, the lines of her face, her lips as they trembled. Each catch phrase seemed to jolt her. He could read her face as a blind man interprets Braille, feeling his way along to the next step in her thought process, leading her back to the crucial information he desired.

"Enhanced, Aubrey. That was the word you used. Concentrate on that word now. Where did it come from? What does it mean? Reach back into that vault, Aubrey, and tell us how the diamonds are enhanced."

The Soviets watched as their subject passed through a range of emotions. Her face became pensive, then frustrated, and then angry. She came up from the experience empty.

"I don't know! I swear to you, I just don't know!"

"You do know! You do know!" Troyansky bellowed.

Aubrey could bear no more. Her fragile composure seemed to crumble under the stress.

"I don't know. I can't say . . . can't tell you anything," she cried, burying her head desperately in her folded arms on the table.

"She's lying," Troyansky snapped.

The KGB man looked down at her as she wept.

"She is not lying. She is incapable of lying while under the influence of the drug. No, no," he contemplated aloud, "it now becomes apparent that Dr. Erhardt was more clever than we had first imagined. He has somehow managed to lock his secret deep inside her, deep in her subconscious mind where not even she can get to it. Not here in Angola, at least."

Troyansky walked away from both Aubrey and Andrei in disgust.

"Where, then? Moscow?"

"Yes, Moscow," Andrei answered simply. "Felipe!" he commanded abruptly. "Escort Miss Erhardt to her quarters. See that she gets a double ration. She is valuable to us. We wouldn't want her to go hungry."

"*Sí*," he responded.

Aubrey rose. The guard took her by the arm as she shuffled dazedly to the doorway.

"Miss Erhardt," she heard Andrei call after her.

She turned. The Russian held a photograph in the air for her to see.

"This man. Do you know him?"

She wondered whether to lie, whether to battle the abandon the drug inspired or yield.

"That is Nick Carter," she uttered. "He is an American businessman I met in Johannesburg."

Vladimir Andrei stared at her for a long moment.

"Thank you. You may return to your quarters."

The guard and his captive left the room. The door shut behind them.

"Andrei," Troyansky rasped, "what do you think?"

"She knows," he answered offhandedly, "but has been programmed not to divulge the information we are after. Instead, it is stored inside her mind as if under lock and key. Perhaps it is a word or phrase—or even the unique pitch of an individual's voice—but whatever it is, our people will find the key to that lock. And when they do, we will have what we need. We will have all the secrets we care to know about."

"Then we must transport her to Moscow immediately. It is too dangerous here. She could be killed."

The KGB agent sat back in his chair. He lifted his heavy boots into the air. They came to rest atop the conference table.

"Agreed," he sighed. "Certainly a psychologist will succeed where we have failed. It must be done—and soon. I have a war to run."

Boris Troyansky smiled, pleased at the potential for success that still lay ahead. He had done what he could. Now it was someone else's responsibility to wrest the crucial data from the South African girl. Vladimir Andrei did not smile, but anxiously clutched the photograph of the American agent in his right hand. Neither said a word as he placed the photo on the table. The gemologist wondered at his comrade's sudden seriousness, but his reverie was snapped by the grunts and clucking noises of Colonel Ithena as he entered singing a tribal chant in his native tongue.

The SWAPO leader stood in the doorway, his ivory walking stick held out before him as if he were posing for a photographer. He became suddenly silent as he looked around the room. His black eyes searched the faces of the two men, then stopped as if jolted by the sight of the photograph that lay on the conference table.

"That is him!" he gasped, pointing his ivory stick as if the photo were a living thing. "The white man I saw in my dream!"

An eerie mist clung to the placid waters of the Cunene River by nightfall. The spot they had chosen to cross was a sluggish stretch about one mile west of the heavily guarded bridge. They inflated the three canvas rafts they'd carried in anticipation of the crossing. The group boarded, two men to a raft, with Ian Hardy riding the third raft, which was loaded with the overflow of weapons and supplies.

Silently, Carter and Shea used their long paddles to push the first of the rafts from shore. The current was all but nonexistent at this juncture, a favorite feeding ground for crocodiles that lurked amid its marshy banks waiting for the less cautious among them to take a fatal plunge. Droves of startled water birds took flight as the others followed suit. To the right and left of them, the rocklike backs of hippopotami protruded from the murky black waters.

"Aw, what the hell," Shea grunted at the sight of them, "the Kavangos have fished this river for generations." But as he spoke, his eyes darted to the riverbank where a gathering of twelve-foot crocs played possum.

Behind them, the two remaining rafts followed their course, pulled gently westward by the current. The sounds of wildfowl and insects heightened their awareness of everything around them. Among such symphonies of nature, it was difficult to realize that just one mile east, thousands of SWAPO and FAPLA troops were poised along the Namibian border readying for invasion. A thought crossed Carter's mind as they moved closer to the opposite shore. The native word *namib*, the source of the name Namibia, meant "place of no people." How ironic, he mused, that now thousands of troops from all over the world were assembled in this desolate terrain to do battle over a commodity as esoteric as diamonds.

Shea used a high-intensity flashlight to examine the riverbank as they neared it. Its probe pierced the heavy mist that enveloped them. He examined the area one section at a time.

"Damned crocs are everywhere," he cursed. "If half the population of Angola wasn't upriver, I'd take a submachine gun to all of 'em!"

"What about the Kavango tribesmen?" teased Carter.

"Screw the Kavango tribesmen! These goddamned reptiles are everywhere!"

"Well, just remember there are two more rafts behind us, so make sure the spot you choose is clear."

Carter scanned the bank as it was illuminated. Shea was right; nothing looked safe. At best, some clearings looked less dangerous than others. Finally Shea shook his head in frustration.

"Take her downstream. I can't find nothin' here."

The river was shallow at this point. Carter had been holding the raft steady by planting the oar in the thick silt below. He let it loose, and they drifted downstream another thirty yards before Shea signaled him to stop. Carter spiked the oar into the river's muddy bottom, and the raft stabilized. He beckoned the others to follow.

Shea swept the bank with his flashlight again.

"This is the best we're gonna do, sir. How 'bout we take her in now?"

Carter drew the wooden oar from the water, then guided the raft toward the bank. They took a final look before they hopped over the side, then pulled their canvas craft to the shore. The two remaining rafts came moments later.

"Not as bad as I thought," beamed Ian Hardy, the last to arrive.

His sidekick, Wesson, and Doc Barnes helped him unload supplies as Carter studied maps of the area. The unit was nearly halfway to Cassinga. The town of Xangongo lay west of them, but as circumstances stood, it seemed best to steer clear of the Angolan population as well as the main southern highway. Carter decided to head due north, following the less traversed Lubango road where an occasional village of goat farmers was all they were likely to encounter.

Carter left Shea repacking his knapsack and walked back toward shore to see how the unloading was coming along. In the dim light, he watched Ward and Barnes destroy the first two rafts while Hardy and Wesson emptied the last of them. Carter glanced to the river. From beneath the inky water he could distinguish the shadowy image of a croc as it surfaced, but before he could shout a warning, it rushed toward Wesson.

The splashing sounds alerted the others, but they stood mute, too stunned to react, as the massive reptile lunged at the New Zealander. It clamped its viselike jaws on his lower leg, wrestling the startled mercenary to the ground.

Ian Hardy was less than five steps away. He staggered back instinctively, then stood as if in a trance. Wesson screamed wildly for help as the crocodile dragged him into the river.

"For Chrissake, help him!" Carter bellowed. He grabbed his machete from among the military hardware strewn on the ground, then rushed to the aid of the stricken soldier.

Carter's words were enough to jar Hardy into action. The other New Zealander, who was without a weapon, began pulling at the croc from behind. Once Carter got there, he leaped upon it, stabbing the wide blade of the machete repeatedly into its underbelly. He could feel the reptile's hot blood gushing into his closed fist as it arched its head toward him, Wesson's leg still held in the grip of its massive jaw.

Ward and Barnes had their machine guns raised at this point. The commotion had aroused a group of dozing crocodiles, and it appeared now as if the entire bank had come to life. Both men's weapons blazed as they fired in short, rapid spurts. The solitary splashing sound of just seconds before had escalated to a maddening uproar.

Though Carter could see what was happening around him, his mind was focused on Wesson's survival and nothing else as he plunged the machete again and again into the belly of the huge croc. Finally its jaws relaxed. Peter Wesson scrambled away through the mud like a man possessed. The beast lay on the bank, its insides spilled beside it, dead.

"Let's get the hell out of here!" cried Ward.

Weapons drawn, they collected the remaining equipment as throngs of frenzied crocodiles feasted on the remains of the mutilated beast. The Angolan jungle seemed teeming with every sinister form of nocturnal life, and the men's reactions were instinctive: they ran to safety. Carter looked back just in time to see the largest of the reptiles rip off a meaty section of carcass and carry it off, leaving the others to fight over what remained.

Peter Wesson lay on the ground surrounded by the four of them. Carter used his knife to cut loose his pants leg. The limb was gashed, but not as badly as he'd imagined. It appeared the croc had intended to drown its victim before feasting upon him. Had Carter gotten to him any later, he'd never have survived.

"Barnes, get me some alcohol from the medical kit! Penicillin, too!"

Ian Hardy stood over them.

"I'm sorry," he kept repeating to his stricken countryman. "I didn't see the bloody thing, and when I did, I couldn't believe what was happening . . ."

The New Zealander awaited a response that would not come. He watched as Carter bathed Wesson's wounds in alcohol, then injected him with 100cc's of penicillin.

"That should do it for now," Carter explained, "but we can't make camp here. It's too dangerous. We're going to have to carry him from here on."

Hardy stepped forward.

"I'd like to volunteer first shift, sir."

Carter assessed him as he stood at attention.

"Very good," he answered crisply. "He's your charge, starting immediately."

The pace quickened after crossing the Cunene. All the men had dealt with the hardships of tending to a wounded soldier before, and despite the ugliness of Wesson's wounds, they were mostly superficial. A stretcher was constructed out of canvas so that he could be carried by two men with relative ease, and in fact, the sight of him became the source of a standing joke. With his entire upper torso tattooed and his leg bandaged, once Wesson was able to sit up, he looked like royalty, a bizarre maharaja touring his jungle kingdom. For the time being he was the "bahhs," a reference to the term blacks used when addressing Afrikaaners in South Africa.

The problem of land mines existed throughout Angola, but with the bridge behind them, the odds of encountering them lessened considerably, and they abandoned using the metal detector ten miles beyond the Cunene in the interests of time. Over the next twelve hours they covered more ground than they had the entire day before. Skirting the major town of Xangongo and taking the Lubango highway had also proven advantageous. They encountered virtually no resistance, though none among them was lulled into any false sense of security. The sound of reconnaissance jets too high to see would not allow it. The major thrust of troops were using the southern highway, since the narrow Lubango could never accommodate the troop movements and heavy artillery of SWAPO's formidable invasion force. Carter's question now was, how much time did they have before SWAPO made its move? It was a query he had run through his mind many times before. The answer, he felt, lay in the upcoming United Nations vote. He figured that the Soviets would abstain from any military aggression in order to cast SWAPO as the downtrodden victim with South Africa as its racist suppressor. Since playing on the reactions of outrage at the atrocities commited by South Africa's soldiers-for-hire was instrumental in gaining the votes necessary to win an economic boycott, it would be foolish to lose that edge now. His feeling was that Andrei's people wanted to accomplish both ends: a worldwide propaganda victory for SWAPO with enforcement of the boycott, followed by a military victory in Namibia giving them access to the strategic diamonds at Oranjemund.

If Carter's theory was right, they had time. About twenty-four hours of it.

On the third day at dusk, the men encountered the second of the scores of small villas deserted and in ruins due to terrorist and government fighting. Their first clue as to what lay ahead was an abandoned government disease control station. Stark and square, its concrete walls gave it the appearance of an above-ground fallout shelter. Upon closer examination, they realized that the Marxists' chief antagonists, Jonas Savimbi and his rebels, had been hard at work during the past couple of weeks. The walls were pockmarked with bullets, and the roof had a hole in it, probably caused by a mortar. The broken-down villa that lay several hundred yards down the road was in no better shape. The narrow unpaved road leading to it bore a signpost that read *Nshila wa Lufu*—Death Road. And indeed, the tiny village was in shambles. Of the ten buildings that comprised it, few were left standing, and even those were uninhabitable, their roofs or walls collapsed. The earth around them, too, was shell-scarred and strewn with reeking bodies, bloated and maggot-infested.

Carter and Ward checked out the exploded shacks for survivors or SWAPO terrorists. There were none. Ian Hardy and Doc Barnes moved ahead, reconnoitering the villa as a possible bivouac site while Shea stayed behind with Wesson.

"Hey! Looky here!" Barnes cried. "Mr. Carter, sir! We found somethin'!"

A thousand possibilities passed through Carter's mind as he trotted double-time toward the two men. Their weapons were lowered, so there seemed to be no imminent danger. In less than a minute, he stood at Barnes's side, panting.

"It's a corpse, sir. I think it's one of ours!"

Carter's eyes sank to a trench below. The skeletal remains of a South African soldier lay shrunken and grinning the timeless smile of death.

He was about to ask if they'd found any others when Ian Hardy called out to him.

"Sir! I found some others!"

The four of them walked to a location about twenty-five yards away. Protruding from the ground were the arms and legs of uniformed men buried in shallow graves.

"Uncover them," ordered Carter, a sense of rage and horror shaking him to his very core. Could Aubrey be among them? he wondered.

He looked on stoically as Barnes and Hardy cleared the half foot of earth that blanketed the corpses. After they'd finished, both men stood to the side. Carter stepped toward the four dead soldiers, then knelt in the dirt beside them for a closer examination. All were badly decomposed, indicating they'd been dead for weeks. From their uniforms and dog tags, it was possible to identify them as the reconnaissance team Van der Grif had ordered into Angola nearly a month earlier.

"Search the area! Not just the villa, but the outskirts as well. There!" he said, pointing to the tall grass that covered both sides of the road. "And in the bush and everywhere else around here! Now get to it!"

The men stared at him strangely. There was a level of emotion to his orders that they'd never heard before. It emanated from one central fear linked more to personal feelings than logic. He dreaded that Aubrey would be found killed, if not in this nameless villa, then in the next or the one after that.

When the men returned from their search, they had no additions to their list of casualties. But the news did not give Carter the relief he'd hoped for. Instead it seemed to heighten the tension that had built within him. To know that Aubrey was not here was not to say she was alive; they had simply not found her today, alive or dead.

It was decided they'd set up camp at this villa for the night. Before anyone unpacked, however, the five men remained for a few minutes, viewing the gruesome sight.

"Whaddaya suppose happened here, sir?" asked Hardy.

Carter took the scenario one bit at a time. It was a puzzle that could easily be pieced together. The clues were all around them.

"The way I see it, this villa harbored the SWAPO terrorists who murdered the South African reconnaissance team sent here last month by Van der Grif. The soldiers were buried just where we found them. Word got around, probably through one of the villagers bragging about what they'd done, and Jonas Savimbi heard about it. In retaliation, he and his rebels systematically executed every man, woman, and child in the village."

A hush fell over the group. Mad Dog Shea had been putting a fire together while he listened to Carter. He lit it as the night descended.

"Sweet dreams," he said, extending his arm cordially to the nightmare of corpses and horror around them.

TEN

They were up at dawn to complete the final leg of their journey. Wesson had responded well to the penicillin and was able to walk with the help of another man, usually his fellow New Zealander, Ian Hardy. His rapid recovery speeded their pace so that Carter estimated they'd reach their destination by late afternoon. Maps indicated they were forty miles from the Benguela Railway that bisected southern Angola running west from the seaport of Moçâmedes and east to Menongue. Intelligence passed along to Van der Grif from CIA satellite photos had placed SWAPO headquarters about twenty miles south of Menongue near Cassinga. Realizing that gave the tiny troop a lift that registered in a newfound enthusiasm. Laughs were as plentiful as the jokes that inspired them. A feeling of cautious optimism grew from out of the simple truth that they had made it this far and were still alive.

At midday, Carter decided to alter their course to the more trafficked roads leading to Cassinga. It was, in fact, a stroke of genius, because as they headed northeast toward the coordinates U.S. intelligence had suggested, they encountered a string of half-ton Unimog trucks accompanied by foot soldiers to protect against terrorist ambush. This proved to be the next best thing to a chauffeured ride for Carter's group, because the shipment of military hardware they carried was headed for SWAPO headquarters. The unit maintained a course parallel to the truck caravan for the last five miles of their trek, then split for the mountainous region on the perimeter of the Quifangondo Valley where SWAPO head-quarters had been established.

The feeling of euphoria that accompanied their find was snuffed out like a candle flame as the five of them surveyed the compound below at dusk. The convoy had arrived. A work crew had already begun unloading crates of G3 rifles, Soviet-made mortars, bazookas, and thousands of rounds of ammunition. Though all wore uniforms with arm bands bear-ing the red, green, and blue colors of SWAPO, Carter's darkest fears were confirmed as he viewed the international composition of the forces assembled below them: Angolan, SWAPO, Cuban, and a variety of Namibian and Angolan tribes. It was impossible to judge for sure, but an educated guess put the total number at five thousand troops. If their schedule for invasion was as near as Carter suspected, they could count on at least the same number at the border plus an additional five thousand positioned in key areas of southern Angola.

Shea nudged him.

"I don't like the looks of this, Carter."

He continued his surveillance, observing the valley below through a pair of binoculars.

"Who would? There must be five thousand men down there."

"How 'bout aircraft? Have you noticed the landing strip? I count better than a dozen Macchi 326 GBs. If they knew we were here, they wouldn't have to bother sending men on foot. One copter equipped with a couple of canisters of phosgene and we'd be belly-up inside of thirty minutes. That's what I don't like. I figure it's time to change strategies now or get the hell out of here while we still can."

Carter could feel Ward's hot breath on the back of his neck as the merc stared down over his shoulder. Carter handed him the binoculars.

"Give me a for instance," Carter said.

Shea crouched down next to him.

"See all that equipment down there? Radar, radio transmitters and receivers—the works. My guess is they're going to coordinate the attack from this valley. We saw the troops marching to the border. There's probably at least that many positioned near Oranjemund. If I'm right, there's a map pinned to a wall in one of those buildings with the schedule for the invasion all set up nice and neat. I say we knock out their main transmitter and receiver, and the jig's up. None of these soldiers will know what the hell to do. The invasion will be a mess. The tribal leaders will get to fighting among themselves—the Cubans and Namibians, the Angolans and the Ovambos—and before you know it, they're easy pickin's for a well-disciplined army like South Africa's."

"That's not the point. We're here to take care of Andrei and Ithena. If we do that, SWAPO is faced with a permanent setback. Sure, any disturbance in communications will throw them off schedule, but we want more than a disturbance. We don't want a limb or two this time, Shea—we want their balls!"

Shea was unconvinced. His ardor, Carter was beginning to realize, derived from two sources. The first was a desire to command the raid. The second was a lack of guts.

"You think the South Africans don't know about a buildup like this? They've got high-altitude jets snapping pictures this very minute. Besides that, I ain't no idiot. I know the good ol' U.S. of A. is pitchin' in with satellite photos just in case they missed something. We do it my way and the five of us stand a good chance of livin' to tell about it. Do it your way and we're all dead meat."

"It's not that simple, Shea. You're going to have to take my word on this, but the South African forces won't lift a finger until those troops cross the border. They can't. That's why SWAPO hasn't invaded, and they won't until after a vote regarding economic sanctions against South Africa is taken at the U.N. I realize that's all political and makes no sense to a military man, but that's the simple truth. We've got to go for the jugular while we can. For all we know, the invasion could be launched tomorrow or an hour from now. Postponing it through sabotage just won't cut it. We've been sent here to destroy this movement totally, now and forever!''

Mad Dog Shea showed Carter the surly sneer that had won him his nickname. There was a madness inside him that was as visible as the tattoos that covered Peter Wesson's body.

"Have it your way," he snarled, "but I think you're a damned fool."

Carter watched Shea stomp off in anger. Privately, he wondered how reliable the mercenary would be. His credentials were good, but the code among soldiers-for-hire was not altogether honorable. It rarely took into account the personal idiosyncracies that could lead to insubordination. The gap between cowardice and bravery was often filled over a pitcher of beer in a bar, leaving others very dead while the soldier in question lived to tell his side of the story.

"Barnes!" Carter called out.

He was at Carter's side along with Ward, Wesson, and Hardy within seconds. Shea paced behind them, barely within earshot, brooding sullenly.

"It will be dark in about an hour. How difficult would it be for you to knock out communications down there?"

Barnes grabbed the binoculars from Ward. He gazed into the valley, assessing the possibilities. There were seven buildings, four of them barracks. It appeared as if the communications equipment was housed in just two: one located in the center of the complex, the other off to the southwest corner directly below where they stood.

"That ain't nothin', Mr. Carter, sir. They're guarded, but I can slip a wad of plastic explosives and a detonator in there easy enough. I could have it set off by their own radios. Ward over here could just home in on their frequency. When they send a transmission—*blammo!*—no more equipment, no nothin'! I guarantee it, sir.''

"How about *our* radio transmitter? Can't we detonate it that way? This has got to be neat. No slip ups. There'll be more than just you down there.''

"Sure thing! I'll just set it for a frequency we don't use much. Set it off myself, if you like.''

"Okay! You'll be moving in as soon as it gets dark. One Shot, I want you, Wesson, and Hardy to give him cover, but not until he needs it. If he isn't fired on going down, he sure as hell will be once those two buildings blow.''

Ward nodded his agreement, as did the others.

"Shea!'' Carter turned to him. "How are you at hot wiring cars?''

The mercenary let loose a throaty hack.

"You're lookin' at a former juvenile delinquent.''

"Good. While Barnes is busy blowing their communications systems, I want you to commandeer one of those jeeps parked to the rear of the central building. Any problem with that?''

"No, sir.''

"All right, then. The rest of you listen and listen good. I'm going down there with Barnes. If we're lucky, a couple of our targets will be taken out in the blasts. In case we're not, I'll be down there to finish the job. Now I don't have to tell you that the three of us will be counting on you to help get us out of that snake pit. With Barnes it should be easy. He'll be in, then out and on his way back before the explosives are detonated. Shea and I might not be so lucky. If that's the way it goes down, wait for us as long as possible, then get the hell out. Got that?''

No one disagreed.

"Barnes, how long will it take to plant those explosives?''

"Give me thirty minutes. It ain't plantin' the plastic, it's the guards that're liable to give me trouble.''

"Kill them if you have to. I suggest a small-caliber pistol with silencer.''

Barnes nodded with satisfaction as Carter shot a short, cool glance back at Ward.

"Once the explosives are detonated, we're going to need a lot of backup from this ridge. Ward, I want you and the others to fire as many rounds as you can get off. I want them to think they're taking on a battalion. Pick off anyone that even looks as if they're in a position to fire at us. Check?"

"Check," the three men rumbled in unison.

"Excellent. We'll synchronize our watches. It's 1800 hours now. Barnes, Shea, and I will be making our move at 2000. Barnes, we'll expect the plastic explosives in place by 2030 hours. Shea, you take possession of the jeep by 2040 hours, the time of the explosion. If all goes well, you'll be carting me out of that valley by 2045."

Carter scanned the faces around him.

"Any questions?"

"No, sir," barked Shea.

The four others echoed his response.

"Fine." He grabbed the binoculars from Barnes. "Relax for the next hour or so, because all hell will be breaking loose once we get underway."

The small group split up without a word. It was as if each man carried within him his own cache of memories that was stored and then examined in private moments of uncertainty. Carter watched as they separated now, lying on the ground or perched upon a boulder reflecting in silence on what, if anything, they felt their lives were worth. What price did they place on their existence? The sum Van der Grif offered was ten thousand dollars. Not a king's ransom, but enough for this rare breed of men.

During the short time that remained before their raid into the Quifangondo Valley, Carter had his own chest of memories to open and muse upon as well. Foremost in his mind as he glanced through the binoculars down to the fortress below was Aubrey. He wondered whether she was still alive and, if she were, whether he would find her in Angola. His thoughts were filled with memories of all sorts of events and people, but at that moment there was one hope that seemed to rise and totally fill his mind: he wanted to save Aubrey. He wanted to rescue her and bring her back home to South Africa and safety.

ELEVEN

Carter's watch read 1955 hours. The night had fallen on the arid, mountainous terrain with its customary suddenness.

"It's time."

Barnes, who had been sitting in a lotus position, stretched his long legs, then stood as if it were early morning and not nightfall. Ward, Wesson, Shea, and Hardy gathered around him, their faces blackened with burnt cork so that only the whites of their eyes were visible.

"You all know what has to be done. So let's do it, then get the hell out of this hole before anyone gets hurt."

Carter glanced at his watch.

"Twenty hundred hours."

He watched as each man read the luminous face of his timepiece.

"Check."

"Check."

"Check."

"Check."

Carter stared at each of them for a short, passionate moment.

"Good luck," he said before making his way down the valley's steep northern side, Barnes and Shea following just two short steps behind.

When they reached the halfway point of their descent, Carter turned to the two mercenaries.

"Well, this is it. Barnes, if your plastic has ever blown anything to bits, we're counting on it this time."

"Yes, sir."

"Shea, you know we're all counting on you for a ride out of here. Once those plastic explosives blow, this valley is going to go crazy."

"You can count on me, Carter. I've been here before."

With that, the three of them separated. It was 2005 hours. Carter had just twenty-five minutes to locate and eliminate the leaders of the most crucial invasion of Africa's long and bloody history.

The moonlight was pale as clouds scudded overhead. This was a definite advantage as Carter headed farther down the side of the ridge. They'd all seen the guards who patrolled the area. The seven hangarlike buildings took on a dimension of unreality once he reached the valley basin, somehow looking more like cardboard silhouettes than concrete and steel against the backdrop of Africa's impenetrable, silent blackness.

He glanced over his shoulder. Barnes had progressed about the same distance. In his right hand, tucked between his arm and shoulder, he carried enough nitroglycerin and cellulose nitrate to level at least three of the largest structures. Shea, too, had done well for himself. He had already angled around the west side of the basin and was headed for the enemy's fleet of jeeps and other motorized equipment.

From behind a cluster of boulders, Carter observed the guards nearest to him. They were Angolans chatting in the peculiar patois that earmarked natives from the southern part of the country. It was apparent that the time of invasion was rapidly approaching. Even in the blackness of night, convoy trucks were being loaded and sent out to the border. On the landing strip a huge AN-22 cargo plane was testing its engines, readying for takeoff. The laborers who packed it were singing a native song in the low wail that had characterized the Ovambo tribesmen for generations. Though he couldn't make out the words of the FAPLA soldiers, Carter gathered they were laughing at their singing SWAPO counterparts even though they would be fighting side by side in the hours to come. He slipped past them, then moved toward central headquarters, using the dozens of parked trucks, mobile surface-to-air rocket launchers, and crates for cover.

The entrance to the central headquarters building was guarded by a solitary armed soldier. There were six open windows to the ground-level structure: two to the front, one on each side, and two to the back. Since the guard was patrolling only the entrance, it was not difficult to move around to the back.

Inside, much as Shea had predicted, was a wall map outlining the plans for the invasion. It was to begin that night with intensive aerial bombardment of strategic targets inside Namibia. South African radar and antiaircraft positions were to be pounded until dawn. The invaders would then advance in a three-pronged assault spearheaded by an armored brigade of Cuban and Angolan soldiers. The first of the troops were to converge on the border town of Ondangua, capturing the strategic S3 highway. The second was to seize Windhoek, the capital. The third and largest of the forces, aided by SWAPO soldiers in place among the Ovambos, was to overtake the Oranjemund mine. With Oranjemund in Communist hands, all supplies and reinforcements coming from South Africa could be stopped, effectively isolating both Namibia's capital and most points north of it. Andrei's plan could work, Carter reasoned grimly. The South African Territorial Forces were outnumbered three to one according to the SAI's most optimistic estimates. A coordinated first strike could bring SWAPO the quick and painless initial victory it had been seeking for more than a decade. From there, the strategy was to assume a classic military pattern: divide and conquer. Realizing that much of the country's population sided with SWAPO, Carter could foresee no hope for the South African cause. Namibia and the Oranjemund mine would, in effect, become Soviet turf.

He looked at his wrist. It was 2015 hours. The droning of

the huge plane's engines filled the hot night air. Like armies of ravenous ants readying to overrun the camp and every living thing around it, the enemy's forces appeared voracious. Armed with every weapon in modern warfare's arsenal, it was crucial that this attack be halted.

Carter's eyes returned to his wristwatch: 2018 hours. Barnes would be planting the explosives by now. Shea should be hot wiring one of their jeeps or Land-Rovers for their getaway.

Through the open window Carter watched as the major players of this venture sat and waited impatiently for the go-ahead to launch their squadrons of Russian-supplied Mirage jet fighters over the border. Vladimir Andrei loomed over a radio operator and sipped from a glass of vodka. Ramirez and Kinshasa sat poring over aerial maps at a table. Present, too, was Colonel Theo Ithena. Dressed in a stylish, short-sleeved jacket and ascot, his ivory walking stick in hand, he stood idly like an alien among them. He seemed unconcerned and distracted, almost as if in some kind of trance. At last he spoke in a loud falsetto.

'' 'They shall be attended by boys graced with eternal youth, who to the beholder's eyes will seem like scattered pearls. When you gaze upon that scene you will behold a kingdom blissful and glorious.' ''

It was from the Koran, Carter realized. Ithena's facial expression altered suddenly.

"I don't like what I see, Andrei. I think the guards should be doubled. Tripled. I can see trouble and confusion, and I fear it. Will you not listen to me?"

The Soviet advisor made no attempt to camouflage his annoyance.

"Colonel Ithena, I've listened to your warnings every day for weeks now. In many cases I have heeded your advice, but now I am busy and have no time for your tribal foolishness.''

He called to one of the guards.

"Take Colonel Ithena back to his quarters, Felipe. He is only in the way here.''

130

The soldier took Ithena by the arm. The African leader jerked it away.

"Use force if necessary," the KGB man stated matter-of-factly. "But get him out of here now!"

Ithena's arms were twisted behind him by a second Cuban soldier.

"I will not stand for this! I am Ithena!" he bellowed. *"Ithena! Ithena! Ithena!"* he screamed as if chanting.

The guards pulled him forceably to the door. The African turned to the others abruptly. His eyes were lit like torches.

"Very well!" he threatened. "I have warned you! 'Behold a one who comes from the Garden of Plenty. He is the Angel of Allah whose vengeance shall topple man's Unholy Temple so that not a stone or brick shall remain unturned!' "

The Russian did not attempt an answer, but gestured him away with a wave of his hand.

" 'It is then that the Errant King shall learn to believe, but it shall come too late! *Too late for salvation!*' "

After he had been removed, Andrei paced from one end of the room to the other, agitated by still another of the African leader's tirades. His expression was more vexed than angered, as if something had happened just then that touched him in some strange way and he didn't know why. He threw the sensation off like an article of discarded clothing.

"An odd breed, these African despots. Their brains are filled with the fantasies of children," he sputtered. "You take a man educated in the United States. He rebels when he learns of the disparities between the decadent West and the impoverished Third World, and returns in outrage to his own tiny country. He begins by preaching the tenets of Marxism and earns himself enough popular support to attain a position of power." The KGB man chuckled sardonically as he paced. "Then, suddenly, he is no longer the 'prime minister' or 'president.' No, this does not satisfy the child in him, and so he becomes the spiritual 'guide,' the 'savior' of his people. He lives in a castle while the rest of the population live in huts. He treats his fellow countrymen like cattle while he and his inner circle drive Mercedeses and vacation on the Mediterranean. Posters in airports extoll him as a demigod. He is suddenly transformed into a tyrant, ordering the murder of hundreds of school children who demonstrate in the streets for more food. *More food!* In the guise of liberation, he turns a primitive but happy nation into a medieval hell.'' Andrei shook his head from side to side in frustration. ''Such is the nature of our Colonel Ithena. My government supports him to gain the backing of his SWAPO constituents. To be honest, comrades, if I had him shot tonight, it would save thousands upon thousands of African lives in the long run.'' He clutched his glass of vodka and tossed back the contents. ''Let us begin, then. There is work to be done.''

Carter peered into the stark headquarters as the brains behind the Namibian invasion again approached the dispatcher.

''Radio Moçâmedes. Tell them the planes are ready to strike. We are waiting only to hear their orders.''

The man transmitted the coded call signals, then proceeded to deliver the message. Carter's wrist seemed to be pulsing to the cadence of his watch. It was 2020 hours. With his major targets situated just yards away, he debated whether to make his move. He drew Wilhelmina from her holster. With Barnes and Shea just minutes from setting in motion their segment of the operation, firing on them now would be condemning him and his men to certain death. But here they were, lined up like ducks in a shooting gallery before him: Andrei, Ramirez, and Kinshasa. All were his for the taking. He raised the Luger. A fraction of a second later, the door to the room swung open.

''The plane is ready,'' a black soldier told Andrei.

''Excellent! Get the girl. Tell the pilot he is cleared for takeoff.''

The SWAPO operative saluted. He turned, then left without a word.

Carter's right arm dropped to his side. *The girl.* Could it be? he wondered. Could it be that Aubrey had been held prisoner here all along? He stared at his Luger, and his fingers wrapped more tightly around the weapon. He could not fail. He would not even allow himself to consider the possibility.

The Killmaster moved with caution along the side of the headquarters building, following the soldier as he walked to a small storehouse perhaps seventy feet away. The lieutenant exchanged words with an underling who was stationed at its entrance. No doubt it was being used as a garrison for prisoners. Carter's hunch was confirmed when the door opened. With a guard at her side, Aubrey Erhardt stepped out into the now moonless African night.

A thousand thoughts reverberated through Carter's mind at that moment. The time was 2026 hours—four minutes to Barnes's detonation. Nine minutes from the time Shea was to sweep through the complex by jeep to make good their escape. But here was Aubrey. Within that same period of time she would certainly be boarding the cargo plane. At the slightest hint of a disturbance, the pilot would be barreling down that runway and Aubrey would be out of reach.

Carter fought a battle with himself. The decision was agonizing, but time was short. He had to put personal feelings aside and wait it out. The major thrust of their operation was to stop the SWAPO invasion of Namibia. If it necessitated standing idly by for the four, torturous minutes while Aubrey boarded a plane bound for Moscow, so be it. Andrei's Namibian adventure had to be crushed; the integrity of the mission had to be preserved.

Carter took a step toward the building's back side, then stopped. In the distance, heading down the mountainside, he could make out a military jeep. It churned dust like a tornado as it rushed down into the valley. Something had happened up there, and Carter wasn't the only one clued into the fact. His wary eyes scanned the dark horizon. From inside the headquarters building, Andrei, Ramirez, and Kinshasa ran to the doorway. The door flung open with a crash as anxious observers relayed the news. Over the monotonous hum of the plane's engines, Carter could hear Andrei barking orders to the soldiers around him. Andrei stood in front of the barracks as mystified as the others. All of them watched, paralyzed with surprise, as the jeep screeched to a stop before the Russian. Two SWAPO soldiers jumped from the jeep dragging a bound and beaten man from the back seat. They had captured Anthony "One Shot" Ward.

Carter glanced at his watch. Its luminous face read 2028. In two minutes the Quifangondo Valley would be transformed into a raging cauldron of flames. *Two minutes*. One hundred and twenty seconds that could see their entire plan of operation exposed.

Andrei eyed Ward venomously, then he looked around the valley with a burning intensity. Within seconds, the scores of military personnel who were on alert—and those who had turned in for the night—materialized.

"Nationalists?" asked Ramirez.

"No, no," the KGB man answered, examining the pulverized visage of his captive. "This man is an American," he said in a low, thoughtful whisper.

There was a click of rifle bolts.

"Search the entire area!" Andrei shouted wildly. He turned suddenly to the storehouse where Aubrey and her jailor were standing. "And get the girl on that plane!"

Again Carter's eyes shot to the glowing face of his watch: 2029. He raised Wilhelmina, bracing his shooting hand on his left wrist, and fired. The bullet struck Aubrey's guard in the heart. He fell instantaneously. Andrei stood motionless as he watched the soldier writhe in the dust. Aubrey, realizing this was her last hope for escape, bolted for cover.

Carter's single shot was followed by a barrage of rifle fire from the mountainside. Wesson and Hardy had separated. The sound of their reports rang from two directions, catching at least three of the awestruck soldiers before they had a chance to respond.

"Separate! The shots are coming from above us!" Andrei screamed.

Perhaps fifty soldiers had scattered, working their way into firing positions, when Doc Barnes detonated the first of the explosives. The radio shack went up with a roar that sent everyone within fifty yards reeling to the ground. Carter was already making his way toward Aubrey, who had taken cover, when the second and third explosions sent a shock wave like an earthquake through the valley. Two red and orange balls of fire shot into the black night. The SWAPO forces must have thought the entire South African army was being unleashed as Hardy and Wesson fired relentlessly from the hills above.

The transport plane's engines screamed to a final, furious pitch, then it barreled down the dirt runway. Despite damage caused by the explosions, teams of pilots rushed toward the Impala copters. Two were already in the air, moving away toward the mountains. Carter fired several desperate shots, but it proved useless. Wesson and Hardy were on their own.

Keeping low to the ground, Carter moved toward the storehouse. When he made it to Aubrey, he found her huddling in a dry trench that ran behind the camp. She sprung up at the sight of him, her right arm cocked back, a bayonet clutched in her hand. He raised his Luger. She appeared ready to strike when her terrified expression changed to one of recognition. Her clenched fist relaxed and the weapon dropped to the ground as her arm fell limply to her side.

"Nick! Oh my God, Nick!" she repeated over and over again as she embraced him.

"Easy, Aubrey, easy," he murmured, but his attention was suddenly diverted.

Carter looked behind him to where a rustling sound emanated. He raised his Luger, but it was too late. Vladimir Andrei had the drop on him.

"Carter!" he growled as if the name itself was blasphemy. "I should have known it was you!"

The KGB agent held his Marakov Luger chest-high. A stream of blood trickled down the side of his face from an ugly gash on his forehead. Carter and Aubrey watched, frozen, as Andrei's trigger finger tensed and a thin, twisted smile crossed his lips.

The shot that clapped in the distance was indistinguishable from any one of the others that filled the Quifangondo Valley. But that slug caught the Russian in the back. His index finger pulled one, final time. The shot he fired as he fell to the ground grazed Aubrey's right side. Her hand covered the wound immediately. Carter looked at her, then up to Doc Barnes who was standing some twenty yards behind the fallen KGB man. His fire was returned in an instant by a SWAPO soldier. It caught Barnes in the chest. Clutching Aubrey in his left arm, Carter raised his Luger, firing and killing Barnes's assailant.

"How bad is it?" he asked, raising Aubrey to her feet.

Her face twisted with a spasm of pain.

"I'll be fine."

"Can you walk?"

"I think so."

Carter's eyes sank to his wrist. It was 2034 hours.

"Come on! Hurry!" he urged, leading her toward the prearranged pickup point where Shea was to meet him.

The two ran as best they could along the west side of the complex as rifle and machine gun fire continued to rage. In the confusion, the various contingents that comprised the SWAPO forces had taken to shooting at one another.

Carter surveyed the scene around them, searching through the smoke and wreckage for Shea. Their timing had been close but accurate. He was wondering if Shea, too, had been killed, when suddenly Carter saw him driving a jeep.

"Shea! Shea! Over here!" he yelled over the cacophony of artillery. "Here, Shea!" he shouted. "Here!"

The mercenary had spotted them. They were just twenty yards away. But Carter suddenly knew he wouldn't stop. Instead Shea plowed ahead, pressed low to the steering column as he gunned the engine, making his way up the mountainside in a cloud of dust.

"That son of a bitch!" Carter cursed, watching the vehicle

disappear into the night. "That son of a bitch," he repeated once more in a soft, hopeless whisper.

Aubrey was silent. He couldn't determine the extent of her wound, so he brought her to a nearby bluff at the foot of the mountain where she'd be safe.

"You stay here. Hide among these rocks until I can get back to you. If there's an opportunity, make a break for it and don't hesitate on my account. Head due west toward Moçâmedes. There's a railway there that can take you to safety."

"But where are you going?"

"There's one last bit of business I need to take care of before I can leave."

"Nick, don't be a fool! Please, *please* come with me now, before it's too late!"

Carter handed her Andrei's Luger.

"Here, take this. You may need to use it while I'm gone."

He kissed her gently on the lips.

"Go now! Hide! There's not a moment to waste!"

Holding the Luger awkwardly, Aubrey made her way to the bluff. She turned just in time to see Carter as he dashed back into the erupting valley.

The bedlam of minutes before had not ceased. Helicopters hovered above the mountain range, flying low like vultures searching for carrion. Already the fire from that area had stopped, although round after round of machine gun shots careened through the black valley as fighting continued among the various SWAPO factions. Like sharks in a feeding frenzy, the battle fed on itself, the SWAPO forces destroying one another in the dizzying turmoil.

Before Carter, the three devastated SWAPO buildings smoldered in ruins. Cadres of soldiers struggled to douse what remained of the structures and the equipment inside, but it was futile. Outside the main headquarters, both Kinshasa and Ramirez lay sprawled, bloody and dead, from the second explosion. There was just one man left of the four: Colonel Theo Ithena.

With most of the activity taking place in the mountainous terrain above, Carter slipped back to search the remainder of the complex. He found Ithena inside one of the barracks in his private quarters. When Carter entered, the African leader was frantically going through a wall safe filled with valuables, loading them into a knapsack. Carter's Luger was drawn and trained squarely on him. Ithena looked up, then nodded sagely.

"So you have come at last," he said in an odd, high-pitched voice. "I have been expecting you."

"Come along, Ithena. You have just two choices. Die now, or walk. Personally, I don't give a damn which you choose."

The nominal head of the SWAPO organization smiled cordially. He stuffed the last handfuls of bank notes and jewelry into the canvas bag, then took his ivory walking stick from the table.

"Tell me, Mr. Carter. Does money interest you? Do you like the taste of money?"

He raised the knapsack in the air.

"It is yours if you turn around and leave this room now. Yours. All of it."

"Do you think I came here for money? If you do, you're crazier than I thought."

Ithena lowered the bag. His eyes locked with Carter's.

"Power? If you want power, you could be *bawana* here. Or in Angola. Or Mozambique. I have influence in those places—and in others. In Russia, Mr. Carter, a defector of your caliber could live like royalty."

"Move," Carter snapped.

"Very well, then. I shall go with you."

The African leader took three steps in front of Carter, still smiling the contented little smile that only madmen can manage in moments of terror. He made a motion as if to open the door but whirled around suddenly instead, lunging at Carter with the walking stick that had been converted into a long, very sharp dagger.

Carter fired upon seeing the reflection of its shiny blade.

138

Ithena jabbed twice at the air before two bullets caught him in the abdomen. He fell to one knee. The macabre smile remained on his face even as he lay dying at Carter's feet.

'' 'Behold a one who comes from the Garden of Plenty. He is the Angel of Allah . . .'' he uttered, then died, his eyes wide open and staring at the ceiling.

When Carter made it back to the bluff, Aubrey was waiting.

"Nick, thank God you're safe! I wouldn't have known what to do or where to go without you!"

He knelt beside her, examining the wound. She had ripped her already torn dress open to expose it. The bleeding had stopped, and a crust of dried blood had already formed.

"I think you're going to be all right. Can you walk?"

"From here? I can run!"

Carter smiled, happy just to see her alive.

"Good," he said, helping her to her feet. "If we can get out of here and into the bush by daybreak, there may be a chance of seeing this thing through."

"Was it a success? Back there, in the barracks?"

"Absolutely. Any invasion launched during the next twenty-four hours will be easily handled by the South African Territorial Forces."

Together they made their way out of the Quifangondo Valley. In the distance, helicopters hovered above, probing the mountainside with huge searchlights in search of enemy personnel. Dense gray clouds issued from below the aircraft as canisters of gas were systematically dropped quadrant by quadrant, bursting below them.

"It's only a matter of time before they get to us," Carter said. "We've got to make it out of here and fast!"

Aubrey tried desperately to step up her pace, but it was hopeless. Her wound had reopened with the exertion and was bleeding badly. The copters were relentless in their pursuit. Carter realized that he and Aubrey could not hope to outdistance them. Three quarters of the way up the mountain, they were forced to stop.

"What kind of gas are they dropping?"

"I don't know. But I don't think it's deadly; there's too much risk it would blow back into the valley. Besides, they'll want us alive. Chess pieces in the international game of espionage and all that. You've been through that routine already."

"Then it would be some kind of nerve gas."

"Probably," he said with a sigh. "Something to put us out until we can be rounded up in the morning."

Aubrey lay flat on her back. Her chest was heaving. Carter applied pressure to the open wound on her side with a folded piece of fabric from her dress.

"I suppose it would be a waste of breath to ask that you go on without me."

He nodded.

"What shall we do?"

"We're going to make it to the top of this mountain. We have no choice."

"I can't do it, Nick!"

"You've got to do it!"

He took her arm and placed it over his shoulder.

"Come on now, Aubrey. We've come too far to stop now." He lifted her to her feet. Perhaps one hundred yards away, two Impala copters swept their piercing lights across the mountainside.

"Come on, now—try! You can do it, Aubrey! We'll be safe on the other side! *Safe!* Do you understand?"

She nodded and stumbled forward, leaning her weight on him. Over his shoulder Carter could see the lead craft skip to the next quadrant. It was less than sixty yards away when the first canister of gas hit the ground.

"Duck!" he rasped as the searchlight passed overhead. "Keep down!"

The copter pilot had not seen them. He continued his pursuit up and down the terrain assigned him, dropping the oblong metal disks all along the way.

"He's passed."

Carter stood, then lifted Aubrey to her feet. She took a

step, but her strength was gone. She was drained, exhausted.

"I can't," she gasped. "Nick, you must go on without me."

He tossed her over his shoulder in a fireman's carry.

"Hold your breath," he said through gritted teeth. "We're making a run for it!"

Carter inhaled only when necessary, but even with that, the wafts of gas that drifted toward them proved numbing. Behind him, he saw the second of the two copters hopscotch into the quadrant beyond where the first flew. Carter dropped to the ground as the searchlight passed over them. The fingers of light extended over the mountainside, illuminating its top ridge. Carter struggled to his feet. Safety lay just fifty yards ahead. They had to make it. *Had to make it.* The thought pounded in his brain like a kettle drum. Carrying Aubrey over his shoulder, he ran blindly toward the top, holding his breath as two more canisters were dropped less than thirty yards from them. Carter held the air in his lungs, rushing forward, until they burned for lack of oxygen. *Hold on! Hold on!* his mind throbbed over and over. He pushed forward until his head was spinning. His vision grew blurred. His stamina was nonexistent. It was not his will but his body that failed him. He breathed. The last thing he saw was the mountaintop, incandescent in the light of the Impala's huge, glowing light.

When Carter awakened, it was daybreak and his head was splitting. He shook out the cobwebs, then turned immediately to where Aubrey had been lying. She was gone. He lifted a shaking hand, then ran it over his beard-stubbled face. When he looked up again, there was a man standing over him. Dressed in military khaki with a black beret cocked over his closely cropped hair, Carter recognized him immediately.

The man was Dr. Jonas Savimbi, rebel leader of the Southern Angolan Nationalist Movement.

TWELVE

Savimbi extended his hand. Carter accepted, still groggy with what felt like the worst hangover of his life. Savimbi pulled the Killmaster to his feet with a smile.

"You have been unconscious for some time now, Mr. Sublett."

"How do you know my name?"

The large black man was jovial, apparently amused at Carter's disorientation.

"There will be time to discuss that later."

"Aubrey . . ." The thought came to him on a wave of anxiety.

"Your companion is well, though she suffers the same headache as you."

"How did we get here?"

"A group of my men participated in your attack on SWAPO headquarters yesterday. A very brave group, you and your comrades. Since we shared your wish to, shall we say, frustrate SWAPO's invasion, they helped provide the cover that allowed you and your friend to escape."

"Why should you help stop the invasion?"

"Simple. I despise SWAPO and all that it represents. I am an Ovambo. Ovambos are the real victims of this conflict in Namibia. The terrorists intimidate our people. They cut the throats of those who refuse to shelter and feed them. They abduct our children, then send them back to us as Communists.''

"I suppose I should thank you."

Savimbi shook his head. His serious, brooding eyes turned boyish again.

"That is not necessary. Come—have some coffee. It will help to wake you."

They walked to the center of the rebel bivouac site. It was all makeshift, perhaps a dozen tents with kerosene stoves for cooking. Rifles and several rocket launchers were visible. The camp seemed to house about twenty guerrillas.

"Where are we?"

"Southern Angola. About fifty miles from Menongue. We took you here for your own safety. I trust you have no objections?"

"Where's the woman?"

They approached the largest of the tents. It was Jonas Savimbi's. He threw open a flap of canvas.

"Right here. I thought you might enjoy seeing one another. She awakened only about an hour ago."

"Nick. . ."

Carter rushed to her, wondering if Savimbi had taken note of the name she'd uttered. They embraced.

"Thank God you're all right!" he whispered. "The bullet wound—how is it?"

"Better. Much better. I'm just so happy to see you!"

Carter looked at the rebel leader.

"It was only a flesh wound," Savimbi said. "We have a medical doctor here in camp. He cleaned and treated it while she slept. He promises a rapid recovery."

Carter noticed now that she, like everyone in camp, was dressed in military khaki.

"Is that true?"

Aubrey nodded.

"I see that I was right," Savimbi said and chuckled. "You both were quite anxious to see one another."

Carter smiled.

"Yesterday morning I'd have layed odds that neither of us would be seeing anybody ever again."

Savimbi ambled toward a portable stove where he poured three tin mugs full of thick coffee.

"Here," he said, handing over two cups. "This should help banish your lethargy."

Afterward, Carter and Aubrey left the tent to walk with the rebel leader into the bush beyond the campsite.

"I'm pleased to tell you that your mission yesterday was most successful."

"The invasion was stopped?"

"Technically, it is still in progress. In actuality, it never really began. It seems the Soviets pulled back their air support at the last minute once they'd learned of Colonel Ithena's demise. There's scattered fighting now between the Territorial Forces and SWAPO guerrillas, mostly along the border."

"What about the United Nations?" asked Aubrey. "How did they react?"

"Quite well, actually. It seems the planned invasion had something of a cathartic effect on events internationally. South Africa had proof of military aid given SWAPO by foreign powers in an irrefutable act of aggression. I would say the Soviets came out of it all with—what is the American expression?—egg on their face."

"And the boycott?"

"There was no General Assembly vote. Satellite photos of the buildup along the border changed the opinions of many concerning the question of who are the aggressors in the region. My information is spotty, of course, but sources tell me that both South Africa and SWAPO have agreed to certain concessions. Serious meetings are underway for a diplomatic settlement once a cease-fire is put into effect."

"So it *was* a success! All of it!" Aubrey laughed delightedly. "The invasion was stopped, and the U.N. is negotiating a settlement to the Namibian question. What else could we ask for?"

Savimbi smiled charitably.

"Your own personal freedom," he stated with a sudden, chilling seriousness.

Carter looked up abruptly.

"What are you talking about?"

"As in any movement of this magnitude, you can both appreciate the fact that there are certain factions here in Africa who are most unhappy with what has happened. These factions must be appeased or a true peace can never be achieved. Their displeasure festers. It grows and intensifies until a new organization builds around it, perhaps as dangerous as SWAPO, perhaps even more so. And that is why those factions must be appeased. A villain must be created and then destroyed so that he or she absorbs that frustration."

"We're talking about a scapegoat."

Savimbi did not correct him. "In a manner of speaking."

"And?" Aubrey hastened to ask.

Savimbi reached into his shirt pocket. He withdrew a newspaper clipping, then handed it to Carter.

Written in Africanized Portuguese, the headline translated: *Colonel Theo Ithena Murdered! Killer at Large!*

Beneath the caption was a photo. The name below it was an alias, but the picture, though not perfectly focused, was unmistakable. It was Nick Carter.

Yesterday night in a surprise raid by Jonas Savimbi's dissident rebels, the man called "Savior" was brutally murdered. The body of Colonel Theo Ithena, Leader of the South-West African People's Organization, was found early this morning at SWAPO headquarters in southern Angola. He had been shot twice with an automatic weapon. The man sought for his murder has been identified as Robert Sublett and is thought to be employed by the United States' Central Intelligence Agency. The bodies of seventeen others, including several of the attackers, have been identified by government authorities as Nationalist rebels and known "soldiers-for-hire." President José Eduardo dos Santos has promised a full-scale investigation into the vicious attack. A $15,000 reward has been offered by SWAPO for the capture, dead or alive, of Robert Sublett.

Carter crushed the clipping in his hand.

"That's just great," he snapped. "Now I suppose both the Namibian and Angolan populations are fighting to see who is going to hang me."

"Robert Sublett? How did they get that name?" asked Aubrey.

"It was an alias they gave me for this mission. We all had them. I guess even the South African government is not without its security leaks."

They walked still deeper into the bush. Savimbi was pensive, as was Aubrey.

"What do you suggest, Savimbi? This is your country. What options do I have?"

The rebel leader was quick to answer. His words and approach had been formulated hours before.

"The same as mine. My movements have been restricted to the southern part of Angola for years. I have had sympathizers and supporters here since UNITA lost its bid for power to the present Marxist regime in 1978. They help my cause. They feed my soldiers. They give us money when they can. I haven't seen the capital in seven years. I don't dare. I would be arrested and shot by a firing squad." He chuckled. "Me, the liberator of this country from the Portuguese, held as persona non grata by the Cubans and Russians who run this puppet government. I realized years ago that SWAPO was no better. They fight for liberation from the South Africans when all they can look forward to is worse treatment by the Soviets. But getting back to your question, Mr. . . ."

"Sublett will do for now."

"Very well, Mr. Sublett," Savimbi said. "I would suggest that you do as I have done. Lay low. Keep to a region where you are welcome. To attempt to leave Angola now would be suicide.''

''When, then?''

The black man thought for a moment.

''Maybe never.''

''That's impossible!''

''It may be the only way. Without the isolation this bush offers, you would be captured and executed in a matter of days. If you are an American operative as the newspapers suggest . . .''

''I'm not, so let's drop it.''

''Just as you please, but I would ask you to remember that we are on the same side. They try to make the dispute over Namibia a racial issue, but it isn't. It's political. The CIA was the backbone of UNITA during its early struggles against the Communists here in Angola. I have no quarrel with either you or them, so I ask you in advance to consider the embarrassment your being captured would cause whatever organization you represent.''

''I'm not thinking about that now, Savimbi.''

''What are you thinking about?''

Carter turned to him.

''A way to get the hell out of here and back to South Africa!''

''That would be ill-advised.''

''Don't you understand? I've got to get back—and so does Miss Erhardt,'' he added.

Savimbi's dark eyes ran from Carter to Aubrey, then back again.

''Would you care to explain that remark?''

''No more than to say that it's vital to the interests of both of our countries that she be gotten back to South Africa as soon as possible. True, it's my photo in the newspaper today, but of the two of us, Aubrey is easily the most sought after.''

Savimbi nodded.

''The diamonds at Oranjemund?''

''Exactly. They're the reason behind most of what has

gone on here during the past fifteen days.''

"Then it shall be as you wish. I can arrange for transportation for two as far as Menongue. After that, there will be nothing any of my people can do for you. You are on your own.''

"That's all we're asking.''

It was then that Carter felt Aubrey's hand slip into his. She was trembling.

It was Savimbi himself who took them to Menongue. In a peculiar way, he seemed to relish the company of Americans. During the late seventies, after the Portuguese had left Angola, Jonas Savimbi had participated in a three-way struggle for power against the Communists. The CIA had backed his UNITA movement and still did—at least financially—so that the rebel leader's contact with English-speaking agents had been exciting, even pleasurable. He had also seen events sour for operatives who were "outside" or "deep cover" caseworkers. After dos Santos came to power, several of their covers had been blown, leading to the arrest and execution of those who could not flee the country. Savimbi realized that this was Carter's plight now. He was the hunted. Pursued by both the KGB and G2, private organizations and general population alike, his capture had become more than a matter of law; it was a national obsession.

The military jeep moved along unpaved back roads that were pockmarked by mortar shells. The bush that surrounded them was teeming with animal and insect life, country left undisturbed for generations. Herds of grazing, black-masked gemsboks took flight at the sound of the jeep's coming. Further up the dirt road, they watched as a herd of elephants jammed together to drink from a water hole. The huge animals' discordant cries pierced the dusk amid a barren, wintry backdrop of skeletal mimosa trees and tall, albino grass.

Savimbi was quiet and thoughtful as he drove. Carter could see that he wanted to help them but could do no more. His power extended no farther than the southern region where he and his men battled both SWAPO and Angolan troops alike. To be sure, he was taking a risk transporting them even this far to the railroad in Menongue.

"I would be extremely careful in Menongue," Savimbi cautioned. "There will be many government troops around after what happened yesterday."

"We won't be going into the town itself. You can leave us on the outskirts, near the railway."

"I suppose we're going to be stowaways?" asked Aubrey.

"You've got it. Hobos. The only way to travel."

Aubrey grinned, then touched her fingertips to Carter's chin.

"Well, the beard makes you look the part, I must say."

Savimbi laughed heartily.

"Better to look like a hobo than the photograph in the newspapers, Miss Erhardt. It is a lot healthier."

His point was well taken, Carter thought. The picture identifying him as Robert Sublett was indistinct, and with a beard the likeness became even more vague. If he could just get to Moçâmedes—where it was more populated—they'd have a good chance of making it back to South Africa alive.

"How often does the train run?" asked Aubrey.

Savimbi shrugged.

"It runs when it runs, I'm afraid. There are a handful of passengers as a rule, but the Benguela line carries freight for the most part, occasionally cattle, and sometimes copper from the Katanga province. Now it's used for transporting munitions."

Aubrey turned to Carter.

"Then, how will we—"

"We won't," Carter answered, anticipating the question. "We'll have to see to it that we're ready *whenever* the train makes its way west."

In the rearview mirror, Carter could see Jonas Savimbi's dark eyes cloud with thought. The man was conspicuously silent for a few minutes. At last he spoke, and his eyes were suddenly clear and bright.

"An idea has occurred to me, Mr. Sublett."

"I'm listening."

"About twenty miles outside of Menongue is a small depot where a trackman resides. It is his job to see that the track is clear and to divert the train in the event of sabotage. If I were to take you there, I'm certain a diversion could be arranged to stop the train while you and Miss Erhardt boarded."

"Odd, the same idea had occurred to me," Carter responded. "Except that there's no way the two of us could pull something like that off by ourselves."

"Quite correct. It would take at least three people: one to divert the train while the two others boarded."

Aubrey's blue eyes sparkled with excitement.

"Are you volunteering?" she asked.

The wily rebel's lips formed a smile.

"After all that you have risked, it seems the least I can do." He gunned the jeep's engine. "I would consider it a privilege to aid you in any way that I can."

The depot outside of Menongue was no more than a shack. It was here that the trackman lived, inspecting the railway on a daily basis, running a small diesel-powered cart up and down some two hundred miles of track to the next depot in Chimbemba.

Savimbi stopped the jeep. He raised a pair of field glasses to eye level, then sat gazing into the distance. He handed them to Carter.

"The train should be running with some frequency now. A steady flow of weapons has been arriving from Russian freighters docked in Moçâmedes where they are unloaded, then shipped to central Angola. I would estimate no fewer than two runs back and forth each day."

Carter peered through the binoculars.

"One in the morning and one at night, I would guess."

"Precisely."

"Do you think we'll be able to board tonight?" Aubrey asked.

Carter passed the glasses back to Savimbi. "We have no

choice," he answered her. "Savimbi, do you have access to explosives?"

"You and Miss Erhardt are sitting on enough dynamite to put the Benguela line out of commission for a week."

Carter and Aubrey looked uncomfortably at one another.

"But that is not our aim," Savimbi added. "We want to create a diversion that will stop the train temporarily, and that is what we shall do. Still, it must be done while the train is in sight, otherwise the trackman will radio ahead to detain the train at the main station in Menongue. We want it stopped over there," he said, pointing, "several hundred yards from the depot, so that you can board while it is stationary."

"Then we must separate," Aubrey speculated.

"Yes. The two of you have only to wait in that thicket while I entertain our railroad employee with a little fireworks. Here is a flare," he said, reaching into a wooden crate behind the driver's seat. "When you see the train approaching, set it off toward the north, away from the train, and low to the ground. That will be my signal to detonate the explosives."

Carter took the flare from him. The two of them paused. Each stared into the other's face: bearded, the both of them. Hunted and desperate, all three.

"Thank you, Jonas. Thank you for your help."

Carter shook his hand. Aubrey did the same.

"When we return to South Africa, we shall tell those who can aid your cause all that you have done for us," she promised.

"Good-bye."

"Good-bye for now, Savimbi."

Carter and Aubrey secured their backpacks as the jeep sped around the trackman's quarters in a wide semicircle to avoid detection.

Once in the bush, they sat in a tiny clearing that gave them a good view of the tracks and the surrounding terrain. The stillness enveloped them in its cottony silence. The only sound was the shrill *whirr* of insects in the distance. It was like being on another planet or, perhaps, on another plane of existence. Nature was, simply, present. It neither progressed nor reverted. It was here and it was timeless.

Carter looked at Aubrey. She appeared equally entranced by the magic of their environs.

"Did they treat you badly?" he asked in a hushed voice.

She shrugged. He could see her eyes fill with tears as painful memories streamed through her mind.

"Nick, I thought I'd never see you again. I thought they were going to kill me. Or—or send me to Russia as a prisoner."

"It's okay. Everything's all right now," he said. "Everything's going to be fine, and—trust me—this is all going to seem like a dream once you're back in Johannesburg, an exciting dream that was sometimes bad, but sometimes good as well. Like now. Knowing that we're both alive and well when just hours ago I was certain you were dead."

"Just hold me, Nick. Hold me close to you."

The headlight of the ancient locomotive, refracted by the dense darkness, sent glimmering shafts of light into the sky as it trudged along the tracks of the Benguela line. Carter estimated that the train was doing about fifty miles per hour and was about three miles away. He pulled a flare from his knapsack.

"This is it," he said.

He broke the flare in two, then lit the bottom side. He aimed it due north and at a twenty-degree angle. A tiny jet of fire streamed into the air, settling on the ground several hundred feet away. They watched as the flame danced in the dirt, then petered out.

"What now?" Aubrey asked.

"We wait—first for an explosion, then for the train to stop. When it does, we pick out a car nearest the middle, then board it."

"What if the boxcar is locked?"

Carter smiled.

"Nobody promised first class accommodations. If it's

locked, we climb to the top, then lay on our bellies for the next two hundred miles or so. We've been in worse situations.''

"Yes, I suppose we have.''

The train was in sight.

Neither of them spoke. In the silence, Carter knew that Aubrey was wondering along with him whether Jonas Savimbi would come through. It wouldn't take much to stop the train. A small explosion, just enough to scatter some debris along the tracks, would do. Naturally, the trackman would flag the train down. A cursory search of the area by government soldiers on board would follow. An abortive attempt at sabotage by rebel forces, they would conclude, and then the train would be on its way. But with two more passengers on board.

Savimbi, Savimbi, Carter prayed. *When the hell are you going to set off your fireworks?*

Dr. Jonas Savimbi cut a solitary figure in the shadowy darkness as he buried two sticks of high-density explosives beneath a large pile of rocks and tree limbs. He reached into his pocket for a box of matches. He drew a match from the box, then struck it. He extended his arm toward the fuse. He lit it. He watched the hemp, rolled with gunpowder, to make certain it was lit. Satisfied, he began to rise from his crouched position but stopped abruptly. It was not a verbal command that paralyzed him, but the sound of a rifle bolt clicking. He turned.

"What are you doing?'' a voice croaked.

Behind him stood the trackman, thin and flinty with old age. Savimbi remained frozen as he approached.

"You don't have to answer,'' the old man said with a crafty smile. "I know what you are doing. A fine catch for me,'' he mused in Portuguese. "Now stand up and put your hands in the air! The government militia will be happy to get their hands on one of you bastard rebels after all the trouble you've caused.''

Savimbi stood.

The trackman circled him, carrying a kerosene lantern in his hand. He eyed the rebel warily as he stepped onto the track and waved the lantern in an up and down motion to signal the approaching locomotive.

The circle of light glowed from nearly half a mile down the track, but it appeared as clear as a beacon to Aubrey and Carter as they watched from their position in the bush.

Aubrey nervously wet her lips.

"Do you think he's been captured?"

"I don't know, but there's not a thing we can do about it if he has. Just pray that his plans have changed and that he's safe, then get the hell on board that train once it's stopped."

Aubrey shut her eyes tightly as if to wish away the danger. "God, this is all so terrible! I feel so helpless!"

The locomotive's wheels spinning on the steel rail made the earth reverberate beneath them. A light switched on in the engineer's compartment as the train slowed and the air brakes were applied. They could see the engineer speaking to a group of soldiers as they passed. The wheels suddenly screeched on the track. The eight-car train ground to a squealing halt about seventy yards from them.

"Come on!" Carter called to Aubrey. "It's now or never!"

They left the cover of the bush. Stealthily the two made their way toward the steaming train as it idled, its engine huffing like an aging prizefighter between rounds.

Jonas Savimbi searched the thin, craggy face of the trackman. There was no sign of weakness or even a hint in that stony mask that he could be bribed or reasoned with. His old eyes held a glint of maddened conviction. He had captured one of "them," one of the rebels, on whom all the woes of Angola from disease to economics to banditry on the highways could be blamed.

Savimbi glanced to the pile of rocks behind him. For all his ardor, the trackman seemed unaware of the sputtering fuse that shortened by the second.

"We'll just wait here for the authorities," the trackman said as he continued to wave the lantern. "The train is stopping now. Soon you will be on it, heading for Moçâmedes where you will be tried and then shot as a traitor." He chuckled in satisfaction.

Savimbi cast a sidelong look in the direction of the dynamite.

"You look scared. You are a chicken, too, eh?" the old man needled. "Well, you will pay for all your evil deeds soon, you scum. I only wish—"

Before he could finish the sentence, Savimbi dived to his right, away from the tracks, then rolled and continued rolling as the trackman attempted to take aim with his rifle. The rebel leader had not yet stopped traveling when the flashing blast sounded. Rocks flew high into the air and tree branches took flight as the ground quaked and a thunderous eruption echoed through the night in the desolate southern Angolan bush country.

Savimbi touched his leg where a dull pain throbbed and blood oozed from a deep gash the size of a quarter. He looked to his left where the wiry old man moaned, staring at his severed arm that lay in the dirt beside him.

Savimbi did not take the time to examine his wound or check on the dying trackman. He hobbled away to his jeep hidden in the bush. By the time the soldiers from the train arrived, the old man was dead and the rebel leader had fled, the jeep's engine roaring.

The militia examined the scene perfunctorily. It was not uncommon. Another terrorist bombing.

THIRTEEN

The commotion that ensued was short but crucial. The bulk of military personnel left the train to investigate the incident. The ones who didn't milled anxiously on either side of the eight cars, eyeing the bush around them with weapons drawn while some of the soldiers stood idly by smoking cigarettes and debating its cause.

Their reaction was just what Carter and Aubrey needed. While the back cars were left unguarded, Carter slipped up from behind. He pulled at the steel catch of the third car up the lane, happy to feel it give. It was unlocked. He pushed the door open, boosted Aubrey up over his shoulder and into the freight car, then climbed up after her. The heavy steel door slid closed behind them like the jaws of some enormous animal. The darkness enveloped them.

Carter drew a flashlight from his knapsack, but it wasn't necessary. A circle of intense light opened up on them. They shielded their eyes, naked as specimens to its possessor. They waited. No words were spoken, just a gruff chortle that seemed oddly recognizable. Carter stepped toward the light. A shadowy figure was huddled in an empty corner of the car, surrounded by crates of munitions. He made no attempt to stop Carter's approach. By the time Carter was five feet away, his eyes had adjusted.

157

"You son of a bitch!" Carter snarled, grabbing Eric Shea by the front of his shirt.

"Easy, Carter. I have a gun."

"You left us for dead!"

"It was too risky to stop," he countered, holding the gun up for him to see.

Carter backed off.

"You could have taken us! You could have at least made a pass! You could have done that much!"

Shea straightened his shirt, still training the gun on him.

"I don't get paid to save people. I get paid to fight," Shea said flatly. "You can save all that esprit de corps crap for some jerk like Barnes!"

"Barnes??" Carter repeated. "I thought he was killed! Where is he?"

"Barnes was just wounded. They're holding him prisoner."

"Who? Who's holding him?"

"SWAPO, who else? Who else would want him? Dos Santos is claiming Angola had nothing to do with the invasion. The Russians are swearing up and down that they didn't even know it happened." Again he chortled. It was abrupt and sardonic, more like an odd barking sound than a laugh. "That's a good one, huh?" he asked, waving his hand at the arsenal of Soviet rocket launchers, grenades, and AK-47 rifles that filled the car. "No advance knowledge. They pulled back their air support at the last minute, did you hear?"

Carter ignored the question.

"And the others, Shea? What about them?"

"Dead, most of them—Ward, Hardy, Wesson. I don't know about the rest, and I don't give a damn, either. But *you!*" He nodded admiringly. "You got your men, didn't you? Andrei, Ramirez, even Ithena. A clean sweep. I envy you for that. At least somebody got what they wanted. Me? I ain't even been paid. Not yet, anyway. But maybe it's good that we met—you, me, and the broad." He dipped his head without breaking stride. "No offense, ma'am. Maybe you can fix it up so I'll get paid in South Africa?"

Aubrey had joined Carter. She brushed back her long blond hair.

"You shall receive your money, Mr. Shea. That was the agreement, and my government will stand by it despite your treachery in the Quifangondo Valley."

"Well, thank you, ma'am. Thank you very much. You're a real"—he hesitated—"a real lady."

Shea looked down to the Luger in his right hand.

"I don't suppose I'll be needing this, eh, Carter?"

"No, you won't be needing it now, but understand one thing: we're just stuck here on a train together. Nothing more. If I'd have had a rifle thirty seconds ago, I'd have blown your goddamned head off."

Shea grunted, then slid the Luger into the front of his pants.

"Well, we might as well make ourselves comfortable," Carter said to Aubrey. "It's going to be a long ride."

The locomotive's engine began its northerly trek about five minutes later. The body of the trackman was loaded onto the train. The FAPLA militia returned to their stations with no great ceremony. By the time the train started on its way to Moçâmedes, Carter was sitting in a corner opposite Mad Dog Shea with Aubrey resting comfortably beside him. He and Shea stared at one another in the darkness.

"You're really something, you know that, Carter? Different from most I've met. Like you really believe in what you're doing."

"I do."

"Then you're even crazier than I had you figured. You're smart, ain't you? Educated and all. Don't you know that none of this means nothin'? This fighting over Namibia—it ain't for liberation like SWAPO says. And it ain't to stop the spread of Communism like your people've probably been feeding you. It's for diamonds, Carter. Diamonds and platinum and chromium and a dozen other strategic metals that the corporations in the U.S. and the government of Russia want so bad they can taste it. That all translates into money, Carter. The kind that white-collar crooks steal on paper and muggers hit people over the head for in the streets. Corporations and governments ain't no different. The stakes are bigger, but they're crooks just the same, no better or worse than the rest of 'em.''

"So where does the infamous Mad Dog Shea fit into all of this?"

The mercenary stabbed an index finger into his chest.

"I figure into it as a go-between. The means to an end. A whore, I suppose. But what the hell? Who ain't a whore in the long of it? You see, there's somethin' else about the corporations and governments we ain't talked about yet. They're steeped to their goddamned eyeballs in hypocrisy. They want their enemies out of the way. They want them dead like they never existed, but they can't do it themselves. They got to look like they're aboveboard for the people, real ethical and such.'' He laughed. ''That's where Mad Dog Shea comes in, if you want to know. I've killed men for ten thousand dollars. I've killed men for nothin'. Hell, I'd kill my own mother if I thought there was a good percentage in it.'' Shea's eyes were lit as he appeared on the verge of some near religious revelation. "But I ain't no hypocrite, Carter. A whore? Yes! An animal? Why not? That's why I got the name 'Mad Dog.' *Mad Dog Shea!*''

"You've got a right to your opinion," Carter stated simply.

The mercenary was disappointed. He wanted to talk, and Carter had sold him short. The boil had been lanced and every drop of his sordid philosophy would flow from it tonight.

"But you. You think you're different from me, don't you? But I know better. You killed Ithena. I heard all about it and so has three quarters of this stinking country. You killed Ithena and you'll pay for that in spades, Carter,'' he spat, then he sat leering at Carter across the boxcar. "Smug bastard! Just sit there, huh? Like a priest listenin' to somebody's confession, is that it?"

THE BLUE ICE AFFAIR

"You know something, Shea? You're right about one thing, anyway. You are a whore, and that's what I think makes my stomach turn every time I have to stare into that ugly face of yours. You're a whore because you don't believe in anything. Nothing. Zilch. Not even yourself."

In the thick silence that followed, Carter could feel the energy drain from him. His eyes shut slowly. Shea's did the same. It had been a long and exhausting mission, and it wasn't over yet. As both of them dozed after the bleary-eyed contest of wills, Carter felt Aubrey stir. He thought then, in the drowsy limbo that comes just before deep sleep, that she had probably been awake for the entire time. Her head slid from his lap as both he and Shea succumbed to slumber's beguiling seduction.

"Nick," Aubrey said, nudging him. "Nick, I think we're nearing Moçâmedes."

He immediately shook off any drowsiness. A moment later he was on his feet, the adrenaline of the previous days still very much in evidence.

"You're right. We'd better make our move now or it'll be too late."

Carter strode toward Shea, who was asleep. He rolled him over with his boot.

"Time for all good little mercenaries to rise and shine," he chimed.

Shea yawned, then stretched. He cast Carter one of the lethal stares for which he was famous.

"Thanks."

Aubrey tightened the straps of her knapsack. She pulled the lock of the boxcar open from the inside. It rattled noisily as the train moved ahead at a twenty-mile-per-hour clip.

"It's grassy below us," she called over the wind and clamor. "Perhaps I should go now."

Carter moved up behind her.

"Try to hit the ground on your side. Keep your body loose and roll with the force of the fall."

She nodded.

Carter yanked the heavy steel door to the side, and it opened about three feet, more than enough for a person to fit through comfortably. He set himself directly behind Aubrey with Shea behind him.

"Go!" he hollered.

She jumped. Carter followed, then Shea. They hit the ground within seconds of one another. Aubrey's choice had been a good one. They rolled down a grassy knoll like kids playing in a park. One by one, each stood. Satisfied that no one had sustained any injuries, they stood silent for a few moments to regain their senses. Carter looked to Aubrey as she brushed her clothes clean. Shea had already arranged his backpack, and a broad grin crossed his hard features.

"Well, this is where we part company, Carter. You and the broad will be a little slow for my taste. Besides, I don't think you're the safest guy to be traveling with these days, if you catch my drift."

Carter was silent.

"Oh," he added as if an afterthought, "when they catch you, they'll kill you. Cut out your entrails while you're hangin'. Slow and painful. That's the way they do it here in Angola. I thought you might like to know."

They watched as Mad Dog Shea marched off in a northerly direction, whistling as he went.

"Charming man," said Carter, tightening the strap of his knapsack.

The stretch of terrain leading into Moçâmedes was desolate but easily crossed. It took them two hours to cover the twelve miles that put them at the city's outskirts. There, the relatively modern buildings of Angola's largest seaport seemed to materialize from out of nowhere. Jonas Savimbi had passed along the name of a British exporter who he promised would help get them out of the country. His name was Jonathan Creely, and the place he was most likely to be found was a nightspot called Bouncing Betty's.

Once in town, he and Aubrey took a room not far from the docks. In this underground society of sailors, smugglers, and foreign agents, no identification was requested. No identification was volunteered. They had Angolan currency. They appeared not to be troublemakers. That was that. The two put their scant belongings in the drab little room, washed up, then headed for the docks to find their contact.

Bouncing Betty's, while far from being any showcase of Angolan sophistication, was not the den that Carter had expected. Though it was located just a few hundred yards from the port, it was more of a cabaret than a low-life bar, complete with tables, private booths, and entertainment. As they entered, a female singer crooned a Spanish pop song accompanied by a three-piece band. The squat black bouncer who stood at the doorway was built powerfully, nearly as wide as he was tall. His large, belligerent eyes traveled up and down both Aubrey and Carter. Satisfied, he raised a meaty hand, then motioned them along inside. Before them lay a semicircle of tables set up around the bar and an oblong platform that served as a stage. The place was only one-quarter full. Its patrons were a mixture of government officials, foreign businessmen, and the local African elite.

Carter bent low behind Aubrey as eyes lifted from tabletops and the stage to them. Carter's beard was full, and his hair was combed straight back in the manner of most African whites. He was praying that no one would recognize him from the recently published newspaper photo.

They sat at a table for two in the back of the place. It was Bouncing Betty herself who sauntered over to take their order. She looked to be in her late forties and of Portuguese descent. Her nickname, bestowed upon her by an American, was entirely appropriate. Her enormous, tawny breasts quaked like overripe melons beneath a sheer, low-cut blouse that barely covered her upper torso.

"Yes?" she asked blandly.

"Scotch. Wine for the lady."

Bouncing Betty nodded. Carter took hold of her hand as she started for the bar. He placed a ten-rand note into her palm. Exercising no great degree of discretion, she unfolded the note in front of him. Her face became animated at the sight of foreign currency, a prize in Angola where the inflation rate tops fifty percent.

"I need to see Jonathan Creely. Do you know where he is?"

Again she nodded, but this time with a sage expression that told Carter she knew the man well.

"Creely here. He here tonight."

"I need to speak with him."

"I tell Creely. Who are you? He will want to know."

"A businessman from the United States. He doesn't know me. A friend of his sent me."

"I say that," she promised.

Carter watched Bouncing Betty leave for the bar. She whispered something to the bartender who looked to their table, then poured two drinks without reaction. Then Betty disappeared to the back of the room and went through a door marked Private.

Carter's attention focused on the stage where the singer began a tinny rendition of "What I Did for Love." He looked around the room perfunctorily. It was amazing to watch the pairs of eyes dart from one table to the next. The tension was so thick one could touch it. Spies watching spies. Drug dealers furtively observing government agents. Local patrons nervously sipping their drinks as if expecting to be detained for questioning before the song ended. This was city life in Angola. Terrorist bombings, infiltration of government agencies by Cuban and Russian intelligence, and surveillance of the local community by plainclothes secret police had turned this club and, indeed, every public meeting place into a pit of paranoia. The singer sang to no one. The tables, devoid of conversation or laughter, made the word "trust" seem like some relic of a past civilization. Mail was opened and censored by authorities as a matter of course. The hotel telephone where foreigners stayed were tapped without pretense. It was a country of people desperate with uncertainty.

"I'm afraid, Nick," Aubrey confided.

She slid her hand across the table and placed it in his.

"This is the only choice we have. Nobody ever said it would be easy."

"Can she be trusted?"

"No."

"Where do you think she went?"

"To get Creely, I hope. If not Creely, the police. In that case, we've got a big problem."

"Do you have your gun?"

"You bet."

She smiled thinly.

"You know, with that beard, I'm not certain even I could recognize you."

"Very reassuring."

Filled with anxiety, they both watched the door to the back of Bouncing Betty's, wondering who would emerge. Carter comforted himself with the realization that their hostess had been around for the better part of a decade. Since the careers of informers are generally short-lived, past experience suggested that she was the smart, quiet type. Pay off the local militia. Stay away from drugs and politics. Policies that survivors learned to live by in the topsy-turvy environs of the Third World.

When the door finally opened, Carter was relieved to witness the sight of those two jiggling, pendulous breasts as Bouncing Betty reentered the bistro. She plucked two drinks from the bar, then wove her way on spike heels toward their table.

She slammed down the two glasses.

"He won't see you. Says he don't know no American and he don't want to know one."

"But he must see us!" Aubrey objected.

Betty shook her head.

"Nobody got to do nothing. Nobody must do nothing at Bouncing Betty's."

Aubrey looked across the table, devastated.

Betty put her weight back on one heel.

"That be two dollars, Mr. American Businessman," she snapped, extending her palm.

Carter handed her the money, not bothering to attempt to change her mind. It would be no use. Once a woman like Betty had resolved a situation to her satisfaction, reason and even bribery were out of the question. Aubrey watched her back blend into the crowd of patrons around the bar.

"What now?"

"If Creely won't come to me, I guess I'll have to go to him."

"How?"

"He's around. She told us that already. It looks like I'll just have to go search for him. Do you think you'll be all right alone?"

Aubrey shrugged. "After everything that's gone on, I think I can cope with just about anything now."

Carter stroked the side of her face with his fingertips.

"Your papers are in order. No one will bother you; Betty and that gorilla at the door will see to that."

Outside, the night was humid and close with the stench of stagnant water. Carter reconnoitered Bouncing Betty's. The bouncer inside seemed to be the only security. The structure was three stories high, not unlike a large house that at some point had been converted for commercial use. The first floor was occupied by the nightclub while the upper two floors housed rooms for prostitutes and sailors on layovers. Carter was convinced that Jonathan Creely was in the building somewhere above.

He circled around to the back. The roof of the first floor jutted out like a ridge from the remaining two levels at a height of about twelve feet. It could be worse, he thought. The back door to the kitchen was open. Inside, he could hear the banter of cooks and waiters talking and joking among themselves. Carter rolled an empty beer keg toward the lower roof. He climbed on top of it, then jumped up, grabbing hold of the roof's wooden gutter. He lifted himself as if doing a chin-up onto the tarred roof. He listened for the sound of a commotion below. None came. The chatter of the kitchen help continued in the same singsong manner as before. He had made it this far undetected.

Of the four sets of windows on the second floor, only one was unlit. Carter chose this for his point of entry. He drew Wilhelmina from her holster, then crawled cautiously toward it. The window was covered with a gauzelike mosquito netting. He peered through it and into the room. It was dark, but he could make out an empty, unmade bed. That was enough for him. He ripped the netting loose, then climbed inside. Gun drawn, he stood silent. Nothing. Not a sound. *So far so good*, he thought. With luck, he could pass from here on as one of Bouncing Betty's clients. *With luck*, he reminded himself, slipping the Luger back into its holster.

Carter opened the door a crack. Outside in the corridor, he could hear the voice of a woman complaining loudly. He poked his head out in time to hear the climax of her verbal assault, a one-sided debate between her and a thin black man. From what Carter could discern, it was over money. At last the man had had enough. He reached into his pocket and handed her a piece of silver. The woman studied the coin, bit into it, then examined the coin again. It was real, she decided, taking hold of his arm. "Oooh, baby, baby," she cooed in Portuguese as she led him into the room.

Once the hallway was clear, Carter left the room confident that there were now only two possibilities. If Creely were on this floor, he was in one of the two remaining rooms. He also knew that his contact was British and therefore spoke English. Could it be that just a tap on the door and a brief introduction would get him the audience he so desperately needed? Carter approached the door to the left of him. He rapped lightly upon it.

"Creely?" he said, not attempting to disguise his desperation. "Jonathan Creely?"

"Come in, come in," the unmistakable voice of an Englishman replied.

Carter opened the door. A group of five men looked up

from the card table where a half-empty bottle of gin rested.

"Well?"

"Are you Jonathan Creely?"

"That's my name," the thin, bug-eyed man replied.

"I need to talk to you. It's urgent."

The Englishman laughed out loud.

"Urgent? Who are you?"

"That's unimportant."

"Well, it's important to *me!*" He turned to one of his pals. "Have Robbie throw this man out of here, will you?"

"I ain't got to," his cohort replied.

Creely glanced in Carter's direction and beyond. He smiled. Carter followed his eyes, half turning, but it was too late. Robbie, the bouncer, grabbed him from behind in a bear hug that emptied his lungs. The card players returned to their game as he gasped for air. Carter's rib cage felt as if it were cracking. His lungs forced small, choking noises from his mouth. He struggled without success, managing to utter just one word before losing consciousness:

"Savimbi . . ."

The table fell silent. Jonathan Creely paused a thoughtful moment, then shouted, "Robbie! Enough! Leave him here with me."

The bouncer was about to protest.

"Leave him," he repeated icily.

The black man didn't say another word. He dropped Carter to the ground like a bag of cement.

"You no need Robbie no more?"

Creely shook his head.

The bouncer moved to leave, then turned to view Carter's prone body one final time. He grimaced with disappointment, then stomped from the room disgustedly.

Creely watched with great interest as the stranger rose slowly to his feet.

"So you know Jonas Savimbi?"

Carter took a deep breath. His ribs were the kind of sore that would have him remembering this meeting for weeks to come.

"Yeah, I know him. It was Savimbi who sent me here. I need to get out of the country."

He studied Carter with vague acknowledgment, assessing whether to believe him or not.

"Where did you meet?"

"In the south, near Cassinga."

"When?"

"Two days ago. We fought together in the Quifangondo Valley."

"The significance of that is not wasted on me."

The Englishman turned to the others at the table.

"That will be all for now, gentlemen. I suggest you get some air."

The four men looked at one another, then back to him. Carter watched their reactions to gauge how much control Creely really had over the people and activities here and in Moçâmedes.

"I suppose we could do with some more of this," one of them rasped, grabbing the practically empty bottle of gin by its neck. "What say you to a bit of fun with ol' Betty, eh, mates?"

The stony faces and unblinking eyes of seconds before changed into broad, laughing grins. "You'll let us know when you're through?"

The Englishman's bulging eyes followed the last member of the group into the corridor.

"I'll let you know," he answered, still watching as the door was shut and the quartet left for the nightclub below.

Jonathan Creely's voice was clear, his words exacting when he addressed Carter.

"I know who you are, Mr. Sublett. In fact, I was contacted by one of Jonas Savimbi's men only yesterday about you. I also know what you've done, which means nothing to me except to suggest that you need my help very badly."

Creely rose, then walked toward Carter. A quick, intelligent smile crossed his skeletal visage.

"You see, I'm apolitical. That is, I don't give a good goddamn who wins this bloody contest between the rebels and dos Santos—or SWAPO and South Africa, for that matter. I know Savimbi as a friend. He returns my favors by seeing to it that others find it"—he hung on the word—"unprofitable to compete with me in certain areas of business. Do we understand one another?"

"You're going to help me."

"Precisely."

Creely pulled a thick black cigar from the upper pocket of a white shirt that seemed three sizes too large.

"How?" Carter asked.

Creely lit the cigar, taking a long, pensive pull. His tiny chest expanded. He exhaled a stream of gray smoke.

"There's a tramp steamer that passes through Moçâmedes twice a week. The *Kalahari* arrived here yesterday. It will be leaving for Walvis Bay in a matter of hours. Both you and Miss Erhardt can leave with it."

"That simple?"

"That simple. Of course, I know your predicament," he added. "The police here are extremely eager to apprehend Robert Sublett, the killer of Colonel Theo Ithena, and by all accounts you are that man."

Carter said nothing.

"Do you have a passport?"

"Yes."

"Let me see it."

Carter reached into his back pocket, producing the passport, driver's license, and inoculation certificate Van der Grif had given him before leaving Namibia. Creely shuffled through the papers, examining the stamps of validation, dates, and signatures.

"Odd, Jonas said you would be needing a new set of papers, but these seem to be in order and a good thing, too; I couldn't hope to get you these now. Not on such short notice."

"In order? Yeah, if you're looking for a passport to the gallows. Did you notice the name on those papers?"

"I did."

170

Creely held them out to him.

"They're made out to a Yank named James Elliot. He's in the oil business."

Carter grabbed the documents from him, studying them one by one. He smiled wryly.

"Sweet Jesus, you're right."

It was then that Carter realized that Aubrey had switched his identification with Shea's on the train the night before. A sweeter exchange Carter could not imagine.

FOURTEEN

The handful of travelers about to board the *Kalahari* lined up at the gangplank. It was 5:00 A.M., but the early hour didn't make things any easier. FAPLA soldiers checked and rechecked passports while local police rummaged through everyone's baggage. Carter and Aubrey had separated in line, careful not to arouse the suspicion of anyone on the lookout for a man and woman traveling together.

Aubrey was first. A captain in the militia asked her the usual questions. She gave the response echoed by most of the people leaving Angola for the continent's southern region: she had been there on business. Since her papers listed her as a geologist, it was the most believable of explanations; Angola's chief exports were copper, diamonds, and crude oil. Her baggage was naturally devoid of weapons or contraband. They let her pass without difficulty.

Carter was the last member of the seven-man line. The police captain's eyes narrowed as he stepped forward. Carter handed over his papers.

"Name?"

"James Elliot."

"Occupation?"

"I work for an oil company."

The captain studied his passport for a long moment. Above his shirt pocket, Carter read the name Mendosa. The captain's eyes raised from the black and white passport photo speculatively. Creely had managed to replace the photo of Shea with one of Carter.

"You are from the United States?"

"Yes."

"A citizen?"

"Yes."

The captain stared at him with a glint of recognition, perhaps attempting to visualize Carter's face as it would appear clean-shaven.

"You are aware that we are looking for an American?"

"No, I'm not."

"You don't read the newspapers?"

"I speak very little Portuguese, Captain Mendosa. I read less."

He nodded his head slowly, then glanced to the uniformed police official who searched through his luggage. The man shrugged as if to say he had found nothing.

"Seeing that you do not read our newspapers, perhaps I can enlighten you as to what has happened in Angola during the past forty-eight hours. A man—a very important man—named Theo Ithena was assassinated in the southwest region of my country three days ago. The chief suspect is a man answering your description. An American. The traveling time between Cassinga and this port is two days. The killer could easily have made that trip to be here in Moçâmedes today."

"I see."

The captain flashed a testy smile. He plucked at the edge of Carter's passport with his thumb.

"Perhaps you could tell me when it was that you arrived in Moçâmedes."

Carter shot a glance up to the *Kalahari*'s deck where Aubrey waited.

"I've been here for the past week. But I do hope you apprehend this Ithena's assassin. The company I represent has taken a keen interest in doing business with your government in the near future. It would be tragic if all Americans were blamed for the act of a single individual.''

Mendosa's face held the lingering smile of moments before.

''I agree. That would indeed be unfortunate. On the other hand, it is the responsibility of this government to see that Ithena's killer is brought to justice, and to be truthful, I am still not satisfied that you are what you claim to be.''

Carter looked around him. Already the cadre of uniformed police and plainclothesmen present had begun to cluster around him. Atop the gangplank, the steamer's skipper observed the goings-on with detached curiosity. Passengers and crewmen on deck, too, were beginning to take note of the delay.

''I'm sorry. If there's anything else you'd like to know, please feel free to ask me now.''

''I will, Mr. Elliot. You can count on that.'' He pivoted toward a team of soldiers. ''I am afraid I will have to ask that you come along with me for a while. If everything is as you say, you can book passage on the next ship, which will be leaving in two days.''

He gestured to his men, who grabbed Carter by each arm. Carter made no attempt to resist. Behind him, he could hear the *Kalahari*'s skipper order that the gangplank be lifted. An entourage of militia, with Carter at its core, approached the pocket of military jeeps that had sealed off the boarding area. Their progress was brought to an abrupt halt when a young private ran to Mendosa with a message. He whispered something that caused the captain to wince. Mendosa nodded, then blurted a few terse words that sent the private trotting back to the jeep. Carter watched as he picked up a transmitter, then radioed Mendosa's response.

The captain brushed past Carter. He stood at the edge of the dock locked in thought as he stared out over the water. Suddenly he turned.

''Hey! You up there!'' he called to the crewmen who had begun to secure the gangplank. ''Lower that ramp! You will

175

have another passenger to Walvis Bay this morning!"

The seamen did as they were ordered. Captain Mendosa strode to the center of the group of soldiers who flanked Carter. They cleared a path without having to be told. The captain stood before Carter.

"You are a lucky man," he said at last. "Ithena's assassin has been found. An American named Robert Sublett. Do you know him?"

"Of course not."

"But you have heard the name?" he prodded.

Carter remained calm.

"I told you. I know nothing about any of this."

Mendosa chortled.

"Of course not. Sublett was shot dead this morning at a poker game not five miles from here."

No one said a word. The impact of the captain's statement had left a vibration in the air.

"Release him!" Mendosa commanded. "Be on your way, Mr. Elliot. And remember to tell your friends in the United States what a fine country you have visited."

Once on board, Carter watched as the crowd of onlookers dispersed. Captain Mendosa and his subordinates piled into jeeps, then left the Moçâmedes harbor.

When Carter turned, Aubrey was standing beside him. They simply stared at one another, then began laughing. A chuckle at first, then with the kind of abandon that only people who have narrowly escaped death can know.

She took his hand and led him to the deck below.

"May I show you to your quarters, Mr. Carter?" she asked with mock formality.

"By all means, Miss Erhardt," he replied with a bow.

As might be expected, the living quarters of the *Kalahari* were cramped and dirty, but happily they discovered a complimentary liter of beer to brighten their otherwise dreary surroundings. It was chilled in a bucket of ice with a note from Jonas Savimbi taped to it. It was a poem:

THE BLUE ICE AFFAIR

In each conscience
seethes the fear of listening to itself.
Someday I come back to Luanda
brave and free with dry eyes.

Carter handed the slip of paper to Aubrey. She read it, then looked up at him, touched by the rebel leader's strength and sincerity.

"Do you think that will ever happen? Do you think Savimbi will ever return to Angola's capital?"

"I don't know. No one could. The only thing I'm sure of is that he's been a friend to us and an ally to our cause. No one ever said the politics of Africa were simple or predictable."

Aubrey became suddenly morose.

Carter poured two glasses of the frothy, Angolan beer. "Here, take this. I think you could use it."

She took the glass into her hand, then took a healthy gulp. The color seemed to return to her face almost immediately.

"We're safe now, aren't we, Nick? No more police? No more soldiers?"

"Yes. Thanks to you and that sleight of hand with the passports on the train."

She giggled.

"I thought you'd approve."

He touched her golden hair. Their eyes locked as he leaned forward, then kissed her deeply.

"Oh, I approve," Carter whispered.

Their bodies clung to one another.

"Make love to me," she uttered desperately, easing herself back onto the bed.

He stared down at her beautiful body. Her khaki blouse was partially unbuttoned revealing the cleavage between her breasts. Her blond hair lay massed beneath her head as her blue eyes swam in the dreamy rapture of surrender.

Carter undid the remaining buttons. Her blouse fell open. He touched the tip of his tongue to the nipple of one breast, then to the other. She made a sound deep in her throat as he opened the fastener on her waistband. He pressed the palm of his hand against the warmth between her thighs. The intensity of their passion registered on her face, which glowed with an almost unbearable pleasure. Her mouth formed the shape of an O.

"I want you to feel me inside you now," said Carter, his voice shaking with urgency. "I want you to feel me the way you've never felt a man before."

Tiny sounds emanated from deep within her soul as he took her. They were the sounds of a woman submerged in sensual ecstasy.

Carter's contacts at Walvis Bay were not difficult to identify: two men in light seersucker suits with sunglasses and the kind of fixed, searching stares that seemed to brand men of their profession. They waited patiently as he and Aubrey made their way down the passenger ramp.

"Mr. Carter? Miss Erhardt?" one of them asked. "My name is Darren Mortimer. This is my partner, Christiaan Blancman. We've been sent by Major General Van der Grif to take you back to Pretoria. Would you come with us, please?"

The two SAI men accompanied them to a waiting limousine. Carter and Aubrey entered the spacious back seat and were promptly sandwiched between them. Security. They had orders to take no chances. Aubrey Erhardt had already been abducted for the information she possessed. This time, the SAI was covering all bases. The limousine was armored, the glass bulletproof.

Mortimer turned to them.

"Care for a drink? A cigarette, perhaps?"

"I'll take a cigarette," answered Aubrey.

"A glass of scotch straight up would do me fine," Carter added.

Christiaan Blancman pulled a cigarette from his pack as his partner poured Carter a glass of Chivas.

"Your brand, we understand," he said, holding up the bottle.

"Quite a time you've had of it, eh, Carter? That's what we've all been hearing. To be frank, you're something of a legend among South African Intelligence these days."

Carter took a swig of scotch, then swished it around in his mouth. It tasted good. Its warmth brought a thin smile to his face as he swallowed.

"I do my best," he answered, still savoring the liquor. "I don't imagine things have been any too calm here in South Africa, either."

"Quite the contrary. Events have rather settled over the past couple of days. But I don't guess you've heard, having been away." The agent turned to Aubrey. "Which brings us to you, Miss Erhardt. I understand you were injured during your stay in Angola."

"A flesh wound. Minor, really. It's all but healed now."

"Still, our first stop in Pretoria will be St. Alban's Hospital to have it looked at. Major General Van der Grif was quite explicit about that."

"Meaning what?" Carter asked.

"Meaning that he would like you both to meet him there. A room has been reserved for Miss Erhardt. The two of you will be taken there by ambulance."

"But why?" Aubrey interjected. "I'm perfectly fine."

"What Christiaan is trying to say," Darren Mortimer continued, "is that facilities have been secured for you to undergo certain tests. Some of them are physical and concern your bullet wound. Others are psychological and pertain to more delicate matters. Delicate in terms of national security, I mean."

The limousine fell silent as the agents awaited Aubrey's reaction. She gave them nothing to go by, just a look to indicate she understood the single word that had been left unspoken:

Diamonds.

FIFTEEN

The ambulance pulled up to the patient receiving area at St.
Alban's Hospital with dome lights flashing. Their arrival was
scheduled for the early morning to avoid publicity, but even
amid the stringent security of South Africa, news leaks were
unavoidable. Aubrey was wheeled from the ambulance on a
gurney for authenticity. Carter was ushered along beside her
by a phalanx of SAI agents. A team of television technicians
aimed hand-held VTR cameras and long-stemmed microphones in their direction.

"Mr. Carter! Mr. Carter! May I speak with you for a
moment?"

Their cries were ignored as the entourage entered the
hospital and were escorted to the fourth floor with the same
wordless efficiency. Two SAI agents stood before a room
midway down the corridor. The door swung open as they
arrived, then closed as quickly. Inside stood Major General
Van der Grif, Colonel Coetzee, and a doctor.

Van der Grif rushed to them as Aubrey rose from the
gurney.

"Mr. Carter! Miss Erhardt! Congratulations!" he
beamed, embracing them simultaneously. "It's so good to
see you. There were times"—he hesitated—"there were
days during your mission when I prayed, truly *prayed* that

181

you would return safely. It is a triumph! The entire affair has been like a miracle for everyone concerned!"

"It's good to see you, Karl. There were times when we prayed, too."

The major general took a step back to admire Aubrey.

"You look well, Miss Erhardt. As beautiful as ever."

She smiled uncomfortably.

"You're lying, Major. I must look a fright, but I won't disagree. It's just good to be home again."

"I knew you would feel that way. You are a heroine. You and Mr. Carter, patriots both of you!"

He swiveled toward his associates.

"You remember Colonel Coetzee, and this is Dr. Robeson." He paused to gauge Aubrey's reaction. "The doctor has some questions he would like to ask you, if you have no objections."

"You're not going to have her go through that now," Carter objected.

Dr. Robeson stepped forward. He was a tall, lanky man. He wore a beard that was neatly trimmed, and his demeanor was surprisingly affable despite the web of tension that had suddenly enveloped them.

"I realize that both you and Miss Erhardt are probably exhausted after your ordeal, but that is precisely why we have chosen this time to make our inquiries. I intend to use hypnosis to free her unconscious. You see, the fact that she is now fatigued could prove to be a considerable advantage."

Carter turned to Aubrey.

"Are you well enough to do that? To undergo hypnosis?"

She stared back bravely.

"I think so. It is true I am very tired, but I would like to end this. I want to go to sleep after today knowing that when I awaken, all of this will be over."

Van der Grif clapped his hands together with excitement.

"Very well," he said. "Then it's decided. We shall begin immediately."

182

Carter gave the major general an annoyed look, then turned again to Aubrey.

"Is that what you want?"

She nodded, her eyes closing. "Yes," she said fervently.

"Thank you, Aubrey. May I call you Aubrey?" the doctor asked.

She nodded.

"Please have a seat. Anywhere. The side of the bed will do nicely."

Aubrey walked to the bed and sat obediently. Dr. Robeson stepped toward her. It was apparent now that from the moment they'd entered the stark hospital room, she had been the recipient of all his attention.

He stood before her. Robeson was a kind, gentle man by nature. His sensitivity could be appreciated only after Aubrey gazed into his large brown eyes and saw the warm, unassuming smile he offered. His nose was long and thin, his cheeks drawn as they met his diminutive mouth and jutting jaw.

"I am not here to harm you," he assured her. "To be frank, I have never worked with the SAI before. I am a doctor. I help people. That is my profession. Do you understand?"

Aubrey nodded. It occurred to Carter just then how fatigue made children of everyone, because when Aubrey looked at Robeson, her eyes were as large and trusting as those of a little girl.

"I want you to relax," he said in a soothing monotone. "Let yourself fully relax now, Aubrey. I want you to be very comfortable."

Van der Grif and Coetzee watched in awe as she did exactly as the doctor instructed. His powers of persuasion amazed them all. Aubrey seemed enamored of him and the sounds of his steady, calming voice.

Dr. Robeson took a penlight from his shirt pocket. He directed its beam at the ceiling.

"Look at the light now, Aubrey. Keep watching it . . .

watching. But as you are watching the light, your eyelids are getting heavier and heavier. You are finding it more and more difficult to keep them open. And now your eyelids are feeling so heavy that they want to close . . . *they want to close*," he said with emphasis.

The beam of light passed just above Aubrey's level of vision. Her eyes were raised to view it, and gradually, as the doctor's dulcet tones cajoled her, they began to droop.

"Your eyelids are getting heavier and heavier . . . and now they are beginning to close even though you don't want them to. But they are so heavy you *must* close them. Close them now, Aubrey. Close them . . . close them."

The only person in the room seemed to be Robeson. His will seemed to negate the will of his subject as Aubrey's eyelids gently fell. The doctor shot a look across the room to Van der Grif and Coetzee. She was nearly under, the look told them.

"There now. You are asleep. Finally resting. You are at peace with yourself and all those around you. Is that not so, Aubrey?"

She nodded.

"And your right arm. It is beginning to feel very light. Lighter and lighter, so that you cannot keep it down. Your right arm is beginning to raise now . . . to float upward."

The three observers watched as her right hand raised high into the air.

"And now it is heavy again. It is so heavy that it will drop back down to your side. You can no longer elevate your right arm. It is simply too heavy."

Aubrey's arm fell once again to her side. Van der Grif flicked on a tape recorder.

"You are asleep now, Aubrey. Completely asleep. When I wish to awaken you, I will count to three, then say 'Awaken Aubrey!' and you will awaken. Do you understand?"

"Yes," she responded in a weak, hollow voice.

"Very well, then. Since you are totally asleep, I shall take you back to the time when you were a young girl. Take you back to when your father was alive and you were twelve years old. You are twelve years old now, Aubrey. Do you understand?''

"Yes."

"How old are you?"

"Twelve."

"Is your father alive?"

"Yes."

"Where is he?"

"At work."

"Where does your father work, Aubrey?"

"At the university. He works in a laboratory at the university."

"Does he tell you about the experiments he performs there, Aubrey?"

"Yes."

"What kind of work is he doing?"

"Diamonds," she answered with little-girl certainty. "He experiments with special diamonds that carry light."

All eyes in the room hung on the young woman as she sat on the edge of the bed. Not a sound emanated from anyone as Dr. Robeson paused to formulate his next question.

"Aubrey, does your father tell you secrets about the diamonds? Secrets that only you and he share? That he has instructed you to tell no one else?"

She squirmed. Her hand raised to her mouth as she began to speak, then thought better of it.

"If your father did tell you secrets about the diamonds, you can trust me. He wants me to know, Aubrey. Tell me what he told you about the diamonds."

Aubrey, now acting as a twelve-year-old, seemed disoriented. She fidgeted, then started to speak but faltered in the end.

At last she said, "The secret is how to"—she struggled for the word—"how to *enhance* the blue diamonds. Daddy

185

called it 'doping' them, making them what he called 'super-conductors.' ''

"And how is that done, Aubrey? What method did he use to 'dope' the diamonds?''

There was no response. Instead she shifted her position on the edge of the bed, nervously rubbing her eyes.

"What is the method he used to 'dope' the diamonds, Aubrey? You can trust me. Your father *wants* me to know."

She grimaced.

"I can't tell you. That is, I don't know," she said, still rubbing her eyes. "I can't . . . I don't . . .''

The doctor stared deep into her troubled countenance. She appeared locked in a battle of wills: Robeson's on the one hand, and her father's instructions seared, white-hot and burning, into her young mind on the other.

"You must trust me, Aubrey! It is your father's wish. Now I'll ask you again. How did your father enhance or 'dope' the blue diamonds?''

She shook her head violently from side to side in a frenzy.

"I don't . . . I can't . . . I want to," she pleaded, *"but I can't! Don't you understand? I can't remember!"*

Dr. Robeson swallowed hard. He looked at Aubrey, then to Coetzee and Van der Grif with an expression of grave disappointment before once again gaining control of himself. Suddenly his expression brightened.

"Aubrey," he said, beginning again. "I want you to open your eyes when I instruct you to do so, but remain in a trance. Do you understand?''

"Yes."

"Good. Now open your eyes."

Her eyes flashed open.

"Who do you see, Aubrey?''

"I see you, Dr. Robeson."

"No, you don't, Aubrey. Close your eyes again."

She did.

"Now, when you open them up again I want you to see me

as I really am. You will see your father, Dirk Erhardt.'' He scrutinized her. ''Open your eyes.''

Her eyes opened.

''Who do you see?''

Aubrey studied the man before her. She squinted as if to gain better focus.

''Daddy?''

''Yes. It's me, Aubrey. Daddy.''

Aubrey smiled.

''You've been at work all this time, haven't you, Daddy?''

''Yes,'' the doctor answered. ''I've been at work at the university.''

A smile was stamped on her face.

''I want to see if you remember something, sweetheart. Is that okay?''

''What is it?''

''I want to see if you remember the secret I told you. The secret about my experiments, about how the boron-coated diamonds are 'doped.' ''

''But you know I remember!''

''Yes, I know you remember, but I just want to make certain this one last time. How are the diamonds enhanced?''

''Liquid nitrogen, Daddy. The conductivity of the boron-coated diamonds is enhanced by dropping their temperature to five hundred degrees below zero,'' she said as if by rote. ''They are 'doped' by immersing them into liquid nitrogen.''

The men in the room burst into a spontaneous peel of relieved laughter, then became quiet once more.

''Excellent, Aubrey!'' the doctor congratulated her. ''You are a very bright girl. And I love you, Aubrey. I want you to know that Daddy will always love you.''

''Thank you,'' she said, suddenly sobbing with the ever-so-vague knowledge that the secret she had kept bottled up inside her for more than a decade was now released. ''I love you, too,'' she whispered, tears of joy streaming down the sides of her face.

"Now I want you to close your eyes again, but this time when I ask you to reopen them, you will not see your father, but someone else. A doctor. Dr. Robeson, the physician whom Major Van der Grif introduced you to earlier. Do you understand?"

"Yes."

"Very well. Close your eyes, Aubrey."

She did as she was instructed.

"Now open them again."

Her eyes opened.

"Who am I?"

"Dr. Robeson, of course," she answered.

"That's fine, Aubrey. Now I'm going to count to three. After I do, I will say 'Awaken, Aubrey!' and you will awaken—feeling rested and well. Do you understand?"

"Yes."

"Then I will begin: one . . . two . . . three. *Awaken, Aubrey!*"

At the sound of the phrase, her eyes opened. She looked around as if surprised to see the three men peering curiously in her direction.

"How do you feel?" Dr. Robeson asked.

Aubrey collected herself.

"I feel fine. Did you hypnotize me?"

The doctor nodded. "I did, and you were an excellent subject, I might add."

Aubrey turned in Carter's direction.

"Did you get what you needed? Did I have the information my father wanted to convey?"

"You sure as hell did!" said Carter, barely able to contain his excitement. "You were great! Fantastic!"

Aubrey extended her arms. He rushed to her, rocking her in a crushing embrace.

"I'm so happy, Nick! Just so happy that everything has worked out."

"It's true," said Van der Grif, riding the same crest of

euphoria that had swept over them all. "Maybe everyone involved has come away learning something. And De Beers has its diamonds, the U.S. has its military secrets, and the people of Namibia have their independence."

SIXTEEN

From their vantage point atop the deep and sprawling Oranjemund mine, Carter and Aubrey felt as if they were standing on top of the world. Banks of huge searchlights cut through the night, illuminating the pit and the hundreds of workers who labored by hand and with mechanical equipment. The cool desert air was filled with the sounds of digging as ton upon ton of rock and gravel was cleared to expose the smooth, flat terraces where the diamonds lay embedded.

They stood in silence, gazing down into the mine, their thoughts both very distant and very private. They thought about the mission that had given the U.S. access to the blue diamond reserves in Namibia. They thought about the hope that had been restored since SWAPO and the government of South Africa had come to terms. And they thought about each other.

"I'm going to miss you when you return to the States, Nick," Aubrey said at last.

Her eyes never left the comings and goings of the workers below. Barely discernible, they appeared like tiny black dots as they labored, like ants on an anthill.

Carter turned to her slowly. He took her small hand into his own, and held it tightly. She looked at him. Her large blue eyes were moist. She was as beautiful a woman as he had ever seen.

Aubrey grasped his other hand. She gazed into his eyes. It was as if nothing else existed, just the two of them standing on top of the world.

Carter pulled her nearer and they embraced. In the background, the mine's floodlights shot probes of white light that cut across the black sky like tracers in the night.

He reached into his pocket.

"I brought something along for the occasion. A present."

Aubrey took a step back as he produced a diamond pendant. He placed it around her long, slender neck, then clasped it from behind.

"Oh, Nick, it's beautiful! Just beautiful!" she gasped.

"Call it a souvenir of our time together," he whispered, gathering her again into his arms.

Together they stood in the black night, bathed in the swaths of light that radiated downward, then reflected back up again.

And the diamond shimmered in its setting like a dazzling chip of clear blue ice.

DON'T MISS THE NEXT NEW
NICK CARTER SPY THRILLER

THE MACAO MASSACRE

The meal was forgettable, the entertainment more so. Conversation consisted of a look and a word here and there.

Carter had filled Fancy in on the short ride down the coast, so most of her time was spent rubbernecking every Oriental man in the room. That meant nearly a hundred faces.

By ten the party was breaking up and they had gotten nowhere.

"Want to call it a night?" Ward Christopher asked at last. "We can start in the morning on the first tee. That is, if you think Miss Adams may really be able to spot our man."

Carter sighed and nodded. "You're pretty sure Brown, the dishwasher, wouldn't be able to identify him?

"I'm sure. He wore those big, aviator-type glasses, and

most of the time his face was turned away from the kitchen door windows.''

"If we're leaving," Fancy said, rising, "I'm going to freshen up.''

Carter nodded again. "I'll get the check. We'll meet you at the front door.''

Both of them watched her move through the tables, and then Christopher chuckled. "Pretty lady.''

"Very," Carter said, rising, "and smart.''

They paid the bill and moved into the club's large foyer. Christopher passed his car stub to a runner, then turned to Carter. "I don't suppose you'd care to enlighten me a little further on what's behind all this.''

Carter lit a cigarette and thought. He liked and trusted this police lieutenant. The man was not only a good cop, he was also a savvy one. On impulse, he decided to give Christopher at least the framework.

By the time he had finished, Christopher's already hooded eyes were nearly closed. "Out of my league," he said. "If it's all that big, this guy is a real pro. I doubt we'll have a chance at him.''

"You're probably right, and if we did get him, I doubt if he knows who actually hired him.''

The car arrived and sat idling at the bottom of the steps. Fancy joined them a moment later, and the three of them rode in silence back to the condo.

"Want to come in for a nightcap?''

Christopher shrugged. "Why not?''

Walking to the door, Carter noticed that the cop's seamed face was drawn and his movements were abrupt and jerky, as if his muscles were not responding properly.

"How long have you been a cop, Christopher?''

"Too long. How long have you been . . . whatever you are?''

Carter smiled. "Long enough to have used up about seven of my nine lives.''

Fancy shuddered and they entered the big apartment.

"I'm going to change," she said and veered off into the bedroom.

"You know, of course, that we'll never get this guy," Christopher said, lowering his big frame into a sofa.

"I'll get him," Carter replied. "If not here, somewhere. What would you like to drink?"

"Anything . . . brandy, if you've got it."

"Coming up."

The drinks were poured and Fancy was just entering the room when the window to Carter's left exploded. A shiny object sailed by his head and landed on the carpet in the middle of the room.

All three of them were mesmerized as they watched what looked like the head of a golf club roll directly toward the sofa where Christopher sat.

Suddenly Carter's training and sixth sense clicked in.

"Grenade!" he shouted and dropped like a rock to the floor.

—From **THE MACAO MASSACRE**
A New Nick Carter Spy Thriller
From Charter in March, 1985

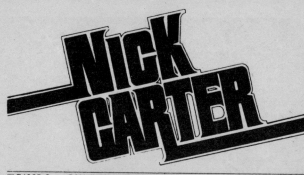

NICK CARTER

☐ 74965-8	**SAN JUAN INFERNO**		$2.50
☐ 71539-7	**RETREAT FOR DEATH**		$2.50
☐ 79073-9	**THE STRONTIUM CODE**		$2.50
☐ 79077-1	**THE SUICIDE SEAT**		$2.25
☐ 82726-8	**TURKISH BLOODBATH**		$2.25
☐ 09157-1	**CARIBBEAN COUP**		$2.50
☐ 14220-6	**DEATH ISLAND**		$2.50
☐ 95935-0	**ZERO-HOUR STRIKE FORCE**		$2.50
☐ 03223-0	**ASSIGNMENT: RIO**		$2.50
☐ 13918-3	**DAY OF THE MAHDI**		$2.50
☐ 14222-2	**DEATH HAND PLAY**		$2.50
☐ 29782-X	**THE GOLDEN BULL**		$2.50
☐ 45520-4	**THE KREMLIN KILL**		$2.50
☐ 52276-9	**THE MAYAN CONNECTION**		$2.50
☐ 10561-0	**CIRCLE OF SCORPIONS**		$2.50
☐ C6861-8	**THE BLUE ICE AFFAIR**		$2.50

Prices may be slightly higher in Canada.

A8

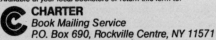